PENGUIN BOOKS

THE EVENING OF ADAM

Alice Thomas Ellis was born in Liverpool before the war and was educated at Bangor Grammar School and Liverpool School of Art. She
is the author of *The Sin Eater* (1977), which received a Welsh Arts
Council Award for a 'book of exceptional merit'; *The Birds of the
Air* (1980), which also won a Welsh Arts Council Award; *The 27th
Kingdom* (1982), which was nominated for the Booker Prize; *The
Other Side of the Fire* (1983); *Unexplained Laughter* (1985), which was
the *Yorkshire Post* Novel of the Year; *The Clothes in the Wardrobe*
(1987), *The Skeleton in the Cupboard* (1988) and *The Fly in the
Ointment* (1989), published in one volume as *The Summerhouse
Trilogy*; *The Inn at the Edge of the World* (1990), which won the 1991
Writers' Guild Award for Best Fiction; *Pillars of Gold* (1992); and *The
Evening of Adam* (1994). She is also co-author, with Dr Tom Pitt-
Aikens, of *Secrets of Strangers* (1986) and *Loss of the Good Authority*
(1989) and the author of *A Welsh Childhood* (1990), an account of
her life growing up in North Wales. All these books are published by
Penguin.

Under her married name (Anna Haycraft), she has written two
cookery books, *Natural Baby Food* and, with Caroline Blackwood,
Darling, You Shouldn't Have Gone to So Much Trouble (1980).

In 1956 she married Colin Haycraft, the former chairman of Duck-
worth publishers, who died in September 1994. She has five children
and lives in London.

D0544058

ALICE THOMAS ELLIS

THE EVENING
of ADAM

PENGUIN BOOKS

PENGUIN BOOKS

Published by the Penguin Group
Penguin Books Ltd, 27 Wrights Lane, London W8 5TZ, England
Penguin Books USA Inc., 375 Hudson Street, New York, New York 10014, USA
Penguin Books Australia Ltd, Ringwood, Victoria, Australia
Penguin Books Canada Ltd, 10 Alcorn Avenue, Toronto, Ontario, Canada M4V 3B2
Penguin Books (NZ) Ltd, 182–190 Wairau Road, Auckland 10, New Zealand

Penguin Books Ltd, Registered Offices: Harmondsworth, Middlesex, England

First published by Viking 1994
Published in Penguin Books 1995
1 3 5 7 9 10 8 6 4 2

'The Cat's Whiskers' was first broadcast as a BBC Radio 4 play, 'Fire in the Attic' was first
published in *Harpers and Queen*, 'The Author and the Air Hostess' in *Cosmopolitan*, 'The
Statue' in the *Spectator*, 'An Arabian Night' in the *Observer* Magazine, 'Judge Nott and the
Dwarf' in *Vogue*, 'An Old-Fashioned Girl' in the *Duncan Lawrie Journal*, 'The Boy Who
Sometimes Did His Homework' in *Country Life* and 'Rats and Rabbits' in the *Irish Times*.

The lines from 'Death is the Fruit' (translated by Kuno Meyer) appear in *Come Hither*,
Walter de la Mare (ed.), copyright © Alfred A. Knopf Inc., 1957

Printed in England by Clays Ltd, St Ives plc

CONTENTS

THE EVENING OF ADAM

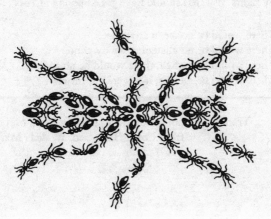

I am Eve, great Adam's wife,
'Tis I that outraged Jesus of old;
'Tis I that robbed my children of Heaven,
By rights 'tis I that should have gone upon the Cross . . .

There would be no ice in any place,
There would be no glistening windy winter,
There would be no hell, there would be no sorrow,
There would be no fear, if it were not for me.

Translated from the Celtic original by Kuno Meyer
from *Come Hither*, ed. W. de la Mare

'What I don't understand,' said Eve, 'is how, while one person is – well, say, looking at the violets in a hedge, somewhere else another person will undoubtedly be torturing a third person to death. Do you see what I mean?'

'Well, not altogether,' said Adam. 'I don't quite see what you mean. No.' He stubbed out a cigarette in his saucer and frowned with assumed concentration.

'At its simplest,' she said, 'what I think is that there is one god of the wild violets and the kittens, and possibly of the sunrise, and another of the torture chambers, and what worries me is, that if I have to follow one I have to follow the one who allows the torture to take place. Do you see?'

'You mean you're a masochist,' he suggested.

'No,' she said, 'that isn't what I mean.'

'Then you mean you don't want to be seen as sentimental,' he said with an air of one concluding an argument.

'Of course I don't,' she said. 'Don't be stupid.'

'Do you mean you don't mean you don't want to seem sentimental?' he asked. 'Or do you mean you don't want to be seen as sentimental? I only ask, because you tend to be a little unclear.' He resented being called stupid.

'I'm not sentimental,' she said.

'All girls are sentimental,' he said, still resentful.

She said nothing. She had not yet learned that there was little to be gained from discussion with a person who neither

3

shares your views, nor wishes to, but she could think of nothing more to say: it was as difficult for her to express what she felt as to describe a dream.

'Do you want the last cake?' he asked, his hand poised.

'Yes,' she said.

'Well, you can't have it,' he told her, and he picked it up and bit it.

'I didn't really want it at all,' she said, watching as he ate hastily, making sure of it.

'You don't want to get fat,' he said, smiling back at her.

'Nor do you,' she said, 'and you've got glacé cherry sticking to your front teeth.'

'I'm not the type who gets fat,' he said.

She looked round the café: apart from themselves it was occupied only by middle-aged ladies in pairs. 'There aren't any students,' she observed, 'except for you.'

'We don't use this place much,' he said, and she wondered why he'd brought her here.

'Are you ashamed of me,' she asked, 'or of the students?'

'You'd find the student dives affected,' he said.

She pondered this, speculating on his opinion of her, the way he perceived her: she knew that he considered her uneducated, but sometimes she thought that perhaps he overrated her intelligence, for he often told her things she couldn't understand – philosophical things that he wanted to say to an appreciative listener, not requiring a response, only unquestioning acceptance and tacit agreement. Her own queries he disregarded as he dismissed her insights. He treated her as those who possessed them treated clever pets, with affection and proprietorial pride, while never taking them as seriously as you would a member of your own species. His expectations of her intelligence were related only to his own needs. He had never had a real pet: nothing furred, scaled or feathered had been permitted in his parents' house.

'Why would I find them affected?' she asked, although she knew already that he had decided that her innocence would be affronted by the self-conscious posturing of his peers.

'They're not your sort of thing,' he said, 'not your sort of thing at all.'

'Do they have beards?' she asked, with what sounded like deliberate naïvety. Hearing herself, she added, 'Because I was thinking about it on the train. I was thinking that beards were always considered a sign of virility and now only thin men who stoop have them, and some young men and tramps – but no elder statesmen, and no royalty except the one who married that big blonde. It's funny how fashions change.' She wished she hadn't used the word 'fashion' since it might give him the impression that she was interested in such things as hem lengths and hats. This would make matters difficult, necessitating further efforts to become visible, to be seen as she was, in truth, rather than the way he wished her to be. She wanted him to love her for what she was. Honesty was a strong constituent in her character, although she sometimes thought this was only because she had an innate dislike of muddle and misunderstanding, and therefore it could not be construed as a virtue. Sometimes, too, she thought that perhaps it was vanity that compelled her to her Cromwellian stand: that anyone insisting that he must be portrayed with all his flaws might not be the type of the simple, no-nonsense soldier-man, but one of such gross conceit that he must bequeath to the watching world even his carbuncles.

'I can't think of any with beards,' he said, having considered her question. 'They're out of style.'

She opened her mouth to say she'd just said that, but decided against it. He hadn't been listening to her.

Two years later nothing had changed very much. They were

married, he was teaching at one of the duller old-fashioned universities, had given up smoking and got rather fat, and she was pregnant. She was no longer in love with him, but then after two years she had never expected to be. She was fond of him, and pregnancy, when she didn't think about it, made her feel like something to do with slow-moving streams through long-grassed meadows, cow-like but cleanly, so she was content up to a point, though with certain reservations.

There had been one disquieting development of which she was not yet aware. He had gradually grown to depend on her: on her daily presence – which was perhaps only to be expected – and also on her scrupulous candour. If she had known this it would have worried her since she had never intended that her honesty should have any purpose but to reveal herself and do away with concealment. She had never meant it to be of use to anyone else. It was merely a tool, like a fly swat, to keep confusion at bay. Now, however, if some biographer had come along to question her husband about her, to inquire whether she had any sterling qualities worth mentioning, he would have cited her honesty. He was now reliant on it, although it would have taken him some time and effort to discover, realize and admit that this was so – supposing he were ever prepared to undertake such an exercise.

'Eve,' he said, one Sunday morning, and then was silent.

'Adam?' she prompted him after a while.

'What?' he said, looking up. 'Oh nothing.' He had been going to tell her about one of his more problematical students, perhaps even ask her advice, but then he had thought that, although she would undoubtedly give him her truthful views on the matter, still maybe she would be unable to perceive the subtleties involved. His opinion of her intelligence had grown increasingly warped as he grew more aware of her honesty.

She spent the morning with the washing-machine, had a

boiled egg and a tomato for lunch, and then went into the garden to sit under the greengage tree and wonder what the future held. The garden was separated from the surrounding fields by a dry, nettle-filled ditch – what, in a grander establishment, would have been called a ha-ha – and, for reasons she had never quite fathomed, it served its purpose. Cows, farm dogs, strangers never leapt over the ditch. She wondered if, when the baby started to crawl, he would fall in it and suffocate in stinging nettles, and whether the ditch itself would present as great a danger as the cows, dogs and strangers would if it were not for the existence of a barrier. Perhaps they should put up a fence or perhaps they would sell this house and move into the town where more civilized hazards prevailed. The gamekeeper had already advised her to uproot the deadly nightshade and the lilies of the valley, anticipating the time when an inquisitive, greedy novice in the world and the garden should range it from border to border, experimenting. Sometimes the thought of how much she would have to teach her child made Eve feel worried and tired. She was ignorant of the ways of babies.

The farmer was driving his tractor round and round the field behind her. Eve had no idea why he was doing this and no real desire to find out, so when he came level with her and stopped for a chat they discussed the political situation rather than the state of the crops, although the farmer did confide that he had had a bad experience only the other day, thus confirming Eve's suspicions that the rural way of life involved many arcane and unforeseeable dangers.

'Jones totalled the muck-spreader,' she told Adam that evening, as they sat under the greengage tree, drinking coffee. 'The tractor hit something, so he baled out, but the muck-spreader was a write-off. Isn't that interesting,' she added, as he did not respond.

'What did he hit?' asked Adam, making an effort.

'Do you know, I didn't ask him,' said Eve. 'I can't think why.'

Adam looked at her warily. She was gazing at the bottom of the garden with an aloof, abstracted air until a mosquito whanged past her face and she struck out at it.

'I'm tired of the country,' she said. 'And it's no place to bring up a child. We should move back to town.'

Adam was startled and – when he had considered for a moment – appalled. 'What do you mean?' he asked. It was surely universally accepted that the countryside provided the best environment for child-rearing. They had never discussed the matter and he had assumed that they were in accord.

'It's unhealthy,' said Eve, 'and dangerous.'

'The baby won't be driving a tractor,' protested Adam.

Eve did not deign to reply.

'What do you mean by unhealthy?' he went on. 'What's dangerous about it?' If he didn't know better he would have thought her capricious, but she had grown more serious of late: sometimes she seemed even morose. Her odd insights, when she expressed them (which she did with less frequency than previously) no longer pleased him with their strangeness, but rather alarmed him.

Eve, if he had asked her, might have explained that this was only to be expected: that a very young and pretty girl uttering truths makes them enchanting, whereas that same girl after some years of marriage will, in all probability, have learned different and deeper truths, and if she has any sense will keep them to herself. Young and pretty girls – Eve might have told him – can carry on any way they like, and should they be open and candid, as well as young and pretty – why, then they are irresistible. But as time goes by, as youth and prettiness begin to fade, the teller of truths seems no longer to carry an air of

8

delightful incongruity but gradually becomes threatening. It was unfortunate that Adam had loved Eve for her honesty since he would, in time, find it unbearable.

Once he had kept her to himself for fear that someone would steal her from him, while now he hesitated to expose his colleagues to her for fear of what she might say. He had made the mistake of imagining that her candour was not incompatible with tact, and was now discovering that nor was it compatible with charity – a far more serious matter when it came to social intercourse. He told people that his wife was given to unstudied utterance, to saying the first thing that came into her head, and he would laugh indulgently.

'The most dangerous thing about it,' said Eve, 'is that it's not the way you think it is. It's ruining my peace of mind.' Here Adam remembered a time when Eve had announced that she was going to give the Master's wife a piece of her mind. He had asked if she was sure she could spare it, and Eve had laughed too. He was not at all convinced that under the same circumstances she would laugh now.

'What do you mean?' he asked again.

'I've got a picture of it,' said Eve, 'in my head. But when I open my eyes and look at it it isn't like that. In my head I see meadows of wild flowers, and clear water, and chickens, and dabbling in the dew makes the milkmaids fair, and dear old Dobbin and Farmer Giles – and public hangings and gibbeted corpses a bit – and ducking stools . . .'

'Sounds idyllic,' interrupted Adam, perversely relieved to think that his wife might, after all, merely be slightly mad. He had no sense, and therefore no fear, of the terrifying honesty of lunacy, believing that truth, sanity and reality represented aspects of the same whole.

'I have been reading of the past,' said Eve. 'I spent all my childhood reading about the past and it has had its effect.'

'What did you ever read,' asked Adam, 'apart from *Winnie the Pooh*?'

'I don't like *Winnie the Pooh*,' said Eve.

'You did once,' said Adam, unwisely.

'No I didn't,' said Eve. 'You're mistaking me for someone else. I liked *Mother Goose*.' She got up and began to clear away the coffee cups.

'I'll do that later,' offered Adam.

Eve didn't pause but, waddling slightly, made for the kitchen door. 'Later isn't any good,' she said, 'when it's got to be done now.'

'Why does it have to be done now?' asked Adam. Eve said nothing. If she had she might have said several things: that the smell of stale coffee sickened her, that the table looked untidy, that moths would founder in the dregs, or simply that later was always too late, especially in domestic matters. That, however, would have sounded puritanical while she wished only to be cutting, not to put herself in a bad light.

In one way – she thought – it would be pleasant to be a bare-footed goose-girl. But only in the story-book way where the tribulations, in most cases, ceased before the goose-girl was too old to care any more. Pale-haired in the dark forests, followed by a flock of devoted fowl, she would endure until she won. Won what? An Adam of her own perhaps. No – that was what happened in real life. Eve stared at a bowl of washing-up water, trying to remember some actual details of a goose-girl story. She could only remember the pictures, but was sure that goose-girls had frequently triumphed over their circumstances.

'I liked Beatrix Potter too,' she told Adam, when she went back into the garden, 'only I never could stand *Winnie the Pooh*. I liked those pictures of cabbages and carrots in Beatrix Potter and I didn't mind all those dressed-up rabbits, but now

I come to think of it I *hated Winnie the Pooh*.' She was not sure why it seemed so important to make this clear to her husband, and he was obviously not interested. 'And I hated *Alice in Wonderland*,' she said. Adam stood up, yawning. Eve nearly divulged that she had enjoyed the *Arabian Nights* but thought better of it. Her urge to be truthful could lead her into remarkably trivial areas.

'Time you were in bed,' said Adam, but Eve knew that what he meant was that he was tired.

She lay awake while Adam slept and the baby explored its environment.

Eve was surprised when the baby was born. She had assumed it would be a boy and it was not. She was also surprised to learn how much pain the body could generate, the involuntary power of muscle, and most surprised of all to realize what love was. It was the quality and intensity of it which disconcerted her. Being Eve, of course, she had to try to explain her feelings.

During the third month of the child's life Adam seriously lost his temper. He had always been self-centred and irascible, but before the baby was born he had considered himself, albeit mistakenly, the centre also of Eve's life. To do him justice, he had tried for a time to regard his changed situation reasonably, telling himself that all new mothers must inevitably become bound up in their offspring. He had tried to make allowances for Eve's distractedness, tiredness and melancholy, until one evening when the baby was asleep he looked up to see that Eve, who was sitting on the sofa, had tears in her eyes. This annoyed him and he demanded to know what she thought she had to cry about. Instead of permitting the tears to fall and appealing for his sympathy, Eve told him. She did not explain that she was suffering from the depression which frequently results from the hormonal disarray consequent upon childbirth, nor that she was exhausted by sleepless nights, nor that she felt they were growing apart. To Eve all that was immaterial. She had, she said, opened her eyes and seen that there was nothing.

'What do you mean *nothing*?' demanded Adam in a towering rage, for this was something worse than ingratitude. 'If you'd stop snivelling and blow your nose, maybe you'd see more clearly.'

'I do see clearly,' said Eve. 'That's the trouble.' Adam concluded that his wife was either mad or correct in her judgement. It was easier to believe the former.

'You're mad,' he said.

Eve did not bother to argue but rose and went to bed.

The next day was Sunday and Adam had asked some people to come for a drink before lunch. The weather stayed fine and he carried bottles and glasses into the garden. The people were not very important – a visiting American professor and his wife, two of his better-bred students and a retired don whose mind was going. Nevertheless, Adam had a word with Eve. 'Eve,' he said, 'I know you've been under a strain . . .'

'No, I haven't,' said Eve.

Adam snapped his mouth and his eyes simultaneously shut for a second, a trick he had when exasperated by a person who either contradicted or failed to comprehend him. 'Whatever the reason, you've been depressed,' he said, 'and I don't want you coming out with a lot of nonsense and boring the Heimlichs with your miseries.'

'I won't say a word,' said Eve, who was not so far removed from ordinary human feeling that she couldn't take offence. She knew that Adam often found her an embarrassment, and she also knew that if it wasn't for his attitude of mingled apprehension and apology many people would accept her at her own valuation. Adam behaved like an inexperienced ringmaster, introducing an exotic and unreliable exhibit to an inattentive audience. If he would leave her alone all would be well.

'Do you mean I shouldn't knee them in the groin when they try to shake hands?' suggested Eve.

'You know what I mean,' said Adam. 'I mean just don't say things like that. Just try and be like everyone else.'

Eve considered this for a moment. 'You can't be like *everyone* else,' she observed. 'You'd look like the cast of *Ben Hur* on fast-forward. I suppose I could watch Mrs Heimlich, and be like her, but I'd get muddled if I tried to be like the professor and the rest of them as well.'

'You know what I mean,' said Adam, his tone slow and slightly ominous. If he had examined his reactions to Eve at this moment he would have found that what he resented most particularly was her lack of respect for him. It had not yet occurred to him that she didn't love him, despite her obvious preference for the baby.

'And try and remember most people aren't very interested in babies,' he said.

'A lot of women are,' said Eve. 'They have to be, really.'

'A lot of women aren't coming,' said Adam, cutting the argument short.

'I know they're not,' said Eve under her breath. 'Most of the women in the world aren't coming. Only one.'

Adam, too, found his last remark ill-expressed and this annoyed him further. He was suffering the anxiety of the host who is about to expose his domestic arrangements to possibly critical view, and Eve was doing nothing to help. 'What are you giving them?' he demanded.

Eve had once had a nanny who, when posed this question,

would respond tersely, 'Shit 'n' sugar.' Eve, however, spoke the truth. 'Olives,' she said, 'and bits of toast with lumpfish roe on, because we can't afford caviar.'

'Nobody can afford caviar these days,' said Adam, angered afresh at what seemed to be the implied complaint.

'That was caviar the other night,' said Eve, 'at the Johnsons. That was beluga.'

'I hate caviar,' said Adam.

'I've done some sardine for you,' said Eve, 'with lemon and black pepper.' But her tone was less conciliatory than matter-of-fact and did nothing to improve his mood.

The students were the first to arrive and Eve welcomed them sensibly. 'You found us all right,' she said. 'The roads are quite clear on a Sunday.'

Adam relaxed sufficiently to pour three glasses of wine without making a fuss about finding the corkscrew, which had been half-concealed behind the bottles. 'Except when they're harvesting,' Eve continued, and Adam stiffened again. 'When they're harvesting,' said Eve, dreamily, 'you can get stuck behind the hay lorry for miles. It's rather peaceful. There's nothing you can do but follow it.'

Adam interrupted. 'You didn't pass Ludo, did you?' he asked. Ludo was the old don who was slowly but surely losing his mind.

'No, I don't think so, did we?' said the students generally, and to each other. 'We didn't notice him. I didn't. Did you? No. I think we'd have noticed if we'd passed him.'

'He will insist on driving himself,' said Adam. 'It's very worrying, but what can you do?' He stopped abruptly and glanced at Eve, who was quite capable of saying that you shouldn't ask him to come for drinks if you were worried about his driving. She smiled when she saw her husband looking at her and he realized she hadn't been listening. 'Anything to eat?' he asked.

Eve looked briefly puzzled. 'I told you,' she said, 'a minute ago. There's . . .'

'Well, shall we have it?' said Adam hastily. 'Shall I help you bring it out?'

'Oh, I see,' said Eve. 'I wasn't going to bring it out yet in case the wasps get in it, but I'll bring the olives.' She went into the cottage and was gone for so long that Adam went to find her.

'What are you doing?' he inquired.

'We've got a plague of ants,' said Eve. 'I've just noticed them. I think they're based under the sink and they come out on expeditions.'

'Well, never mind them now,' said Adam, impatiently. 'We've got guests.'

'You may have guests,' said Eve. 'I've got ants.'

'Don't-be-so-bloody-stupid,' said Adam, whispering. 'Come-on-out-and-behave-like-a-normal-human-being.'

'You don't understand,' said Eve. 'I think they may have got into the light refreshments. I just saw a bit of lumpfish roe move.'

'I don't care,' said Adam. 'Just bring it out and don't mention it. Just come on.' As he passed around the plates it occurred to him that he had been precipitate. He should have told Eve not to say one word about ants, not to suggest that the guests might mistake fish eggs for ants' eggs, not to voice concern for the likely bewilderment of the small creatures. She might say anything. Already she was looking closely at the plate on the table. 'Here are the Heimlichs,' he said, too loudly, as they emerged from the shadowed path into the garden. 'You found us all right.' Then he wished he had let Eve say that. She had sounded quite ordinary and reasonable saying it to the students.

The Heimlichs had, by this time, seen many English country

gardens and grown a little blasé about them. 'I like your lupins,' said Mrs Heimlich.

'And this is a greengage, isn't it?' said the professor, tapping the tree with a rolled-up copy of the *Observer*.

'Oh, you've got a baby,' observed Mrs Heimlich, catching sight of the basket on the garden bench. 'Isn't he *cute*.'

'It's a girl, actually,' said Adam, before his wife could speak.

'So hard to tell when they're so little, isn't it?' said Mrs Heimlich, by way of excuse.

'Not if you know where to look,' said Adam, and stopped, appalled, as he heard himself. It was one of Eve's remarks. She had said it at the christening, thus lowering the tone of the occasion quite unnecessarily.

'That's perfectly true,' agreed Mrs Heimlich, not at all disconcerted. Adam smiled uneasily. A normal woman, he thought, would have responded with distaste, would, at least, have withheld approval.

'Caviar?' he offered.

'I don't care for caviar, thank you,' said Mrs Heimlich, helping herself to an olive. Adam decided he didn't like her. It was quite probable that she would get on well with Eve.

'Devilled sardine?' he suggested sarcastically.

Mrs Heimlich regarded him with an air of mild surprise. 'I'm allergic to seafood,' she said, as though he could have been expected to know that.

Eve listened tranquilly. She had met several educated American ladies and felt quite at home with their assumption that all human beings were equal, were much the same, and therefore should be able to communicate without undue explanation or heart-searching. Adam, she knew, found this unwomanly and unseemly. He thought that women should be modest and – if not exactly mysterious – should keep their mouths shut most of the time, partly because he thought they had nothing to say, but largely because what they did say confounded his expectations. Besides, Adam liked to do the talking.

'Hullo, Ludo,' he said, as the mad don appeared, tottering slightly. 'Eve, here's Ludo.'

Eve was speculating on the possible reaction of Mrs Heimlich were she to become aware of Adam's attitude to the female sex. It would – mused Eve – be entertaining for a moment, but not conducive to a civilized atmosphere: it would disrupt the tenor of an academic English afternoon in the garden. Certainly these were sometimes fraught with ill-feeling, but it was usually occasioned by scholarly disagreement or personality clashes between the males present. At Adam's university, matters were still conducted in a traditional fashion and the ladies passed cucumber sandwiches, if a little desperately (many were on tranquillizers or drank in secret) and discussed among themselves such things as social work and the overwhelming need for the provision of more crèches.

'*Eve*,' said Adam.

'Hullo, Ludo,' said Eve. 'Have a sardine.'

Ludo chose a piece of toast with lumpfish roe on it. A fish egg broke away from the rest and settled on his chin.

'Ludo,' said the students, 'you are a messy old thing. Where's your hanky? Here, let me . . .' They bore him away to a shady corner and a garden seat where they sat him down and fussed about him in a motherly way.

'It's rather touching,' said Mrs Heimlich, 'the way they're so good to each other. Homosexuals.'

Her husband bent an indulgent if faintly nervous glance on her. 'You're not supposed to say that, Nancy,' he observed.

'Don't be ridiculous,' said Mrs Heimlich, consuming a further olive.

'Wine?' asked Adam evenly.

'When I'm very old,' said Eve, 'I'd like to be looked after by a young man or two.'

'Why is that?' asked the professor.

'I don't think they'd beat me up,' said Eve. 'Not if they knew and loved me well. There are grannies in the village who are black and blue because their families thump them for being tiresome.'

'You shouldn't say that,' said Adam. 'You don't know anything about it.'

'Jones told me,' said Eve. 'There's an epidemic of granny-bashing going on. You can hear their old bones crack in the evening when everyone comes home from work, and they want to eat their teas in peace in front of the telly and granny won't get out of the armchair. They seize her by her withered old leg and throw her down on the linoleum.'

Mrs Heimlich looked serious, but not unduly so.

'You should be more careful in what you say,' said Adam, but he was annoyed less by the possibly slanderous aspects of his wife's conversation than by what seemed to him to be its fantastic elements. Why, for instance, did she imagine the village houses to be furnished with linoleum?

'Ludo seems to think there's trouble brewing in Algeria,' remarked the undergraduates, reintroducing themselves into the group and supporting the aged don between them.

'I'm sure he's right,' said Professor Heimlich. 'Islam is on the march.'

'Ludo says fundamentalism in all its forms is undermining the proper bases of authority world-wide, don't you, Ludo? Yes, exactly. That's what Ludo says,' said the undergraduates, setting him carefully down on another chair near the table.

'I'm afraid it's incontrovertible,' agreed the professor, briefly arranging his face in an anxious frown to indicate that he appreciated the gravity of the situation. 'You remember the quote from Yeats . . .'

'"The best lack all conviction while the worst are full of passionate intensity,"' chorused the undergraduates.

'We must never allow ourselves to fall into the trap of believing ourselves to be powerless,' stated Mrs Heimlich, with pious firmness.

'How d'you mean, honey?' inquired the professor. Adam's mouth hung open a little: it struck him as strange to hear a man encouraging his wife to air her views. He did not think Mrs Heimlich particularly stupid (no more than most women) but he could not see that the ideas of *any* woman could be relevant in a discussion not concerned solely with frivolities.

'I mean that if we believe ourselves to be powerless,' said Mrs Heimlich, 'we will have fallen into a trap. The enemy always takes advantage of an adversary's weakness.' The Heimlichs shared a moment of respectful silence as they contemplated this insight.

'I know,' said Eve, and would have continued, but Adam interrupted. 'What did you think of Hudson's piece in the *TLS*?' he asked the professor, loudly. They fell into esoteric discussion, of interest only to those well-versed in their discipline, and left Eve and Mrs Heimlich to amuse themselves with feminine topics.

'How do you put up with him?' asked Mrs Heimlich, never one to beat about the bush.

'I'm not sure,' said Eve. 'I often wonder.'

'You don't have to, you know,' said Mrs Heimlich.

'I do in a way,' said Eve, 'because the baby's small and I'm not qualified to do anything but put up with being married.'

'Stuff and nonsense,' said Mrs Heimlich in an American manner.

'Besides,' said Eve, 'he's not all that bad.' Mrs Heimlich looked dubious. 'Honestly,' said Eve, 'there are a lot of Englishmen who are worse.' Mrs Heimlich looked frankly incredulous.

'I know what you're going to say,' Eve went on. 'You're going to say it's all the fault of the public schools. You're absolutely right of course.'

'I was going to say,' Mrs Heimlich announced vigorously, 'that it's all the fault of English women. If the men are allowed to be arrogant and patronizing, then the women have a lot to answer for, letting them get away with it.'

'I don't mind the arrogance and patronizing so much as how they can't put a washer on a tap,' said Eve. 'I have to do things like that myself, because Adam thinks it's beneath him, and anyway, he wouldn't know how to.'

'Whatever happened to New Man?' asked Mrs Heimlich, but her tone was abstracted and her question rhetorical, requiring no answer apart from a sigh of agreement. Eve supplied this. Mrs Heimlich bent closer and squinted at her through narrowed eyes. 'You're too smart to go on with it for long,' she said. 'I've known a lot of women and I can tell the losers. You're no loser.'

'It's interesting you should say that,' said Eve, 'because I'd have thought I was. I often feel very beaten and pointless. You do feel like that if nobody listens to you.'

'But you're a smart girl,' Mrs Heimlich informed her. 'You've got a brain.'

Adam heard this word and thought it tactless. He glanced nervously at where Ludo sat flanked by his acolytes.

'Ludo says we must all watch Eastern Europe very carefully,' said these young men. 'Don't you, Ludo? He says the collapse of communism is going to leave a dangerous power vacuum. He sees no cause for rejoicing on the part of the West, do you, Ludo?'

Mrs Heimlich and Eve listened in silence until Adam and the professor resumed their conversation. 'Well, I could have told *him* that,' said Eve, when it was safe to speak.

'You've got a brain,' repeated Mrs Heimlich, and Adam twitched.

Eve mused. She supposed it must be true since she had been half-consciously evaluating the guests in the garden and found them wanting. Even Mrs Heimlich, of whom she was growing rather fond, could not be described as a great or original thinker, nor, if she was to be perfectly honest, was Mrs Heimlich terribly interesting. This reflection made Eve feel guilty. 'Have an olive,' she said.

'Would anyone like the last of the caviar?' invited Adam, as he ate it, grimacing slightly.

The baby began to howl.

'There was an ant in that bit,' said Eve.

Mrs Heimlich smiled approvingly.

'Do something about the baby, can't you?' said Adam.

'Why don't *you*?' asked Mrs Heimlich. 'Why don't you do something?'

Adam ignored her.

Eve grew a little irritated with Mrs Heimlich. It wasn't polite of her to point out Adam's deficiencies with such meticulous precision. It wasn't sociable, and it made Eve look a fool. She picked up the baby and carried her under the shade of the greengage tree.

Mrs Heimlich followed.

'He's no good with the baby,' said Eve. 'She doesn't like him.'

'That's terrible,' said Mrs Heimlich, but she spoke placidly, as one who was not greatly surprised.

'I don't think any men are any good with babies,' said Eve, defiantly, putting Mrs Heimlich in a dilemma.

While in her heart of hearts Mrs Heimlich knew this to be broadly true, it was not, at present, received opinion in the circles in which she moved. In these circles it was held that men, if properly counselled, encouraged and supported, would emerge as gentle, as able to express their emotions freely, able to weep without shyness and to engage in warm physical contact with other human beings without necessarily experiencing sexual arousal. She knew all this to be hogwash, but had never quite liked to say so since she adhered not to the orthodox but to the more liberal wing of feminism which allowed that men were human – if imperfectly so – and should not be the targets of too much destructive criticism, as this would be counter-productive. Looking however at Adam, Ludo and the undergraduates, her instinct triumphed. 'Nor do I,' she said.

'Your one seems OK,' said Eve, generous in response. Mrs Heimlich bowed her head slightly in acknowledgement of the tribute. Her one, since he moved in the same social circles as herself, when outside the academic context, knew better than to speak or behave in a traditionally masculine fashion and never threw his weight about or snapped his fingers, while within academia the concept of political correctness was slowly bringing him to the first stages of mental instability, imperceptible as yet to the outsider, but evident to the wife who knew him. A neurotic inability to say what he meant was one of the signs. The outsider might consider such hesitance to be the mark of the thoughtful, measured mentor, but his wife knew it was the result of fearing he might open his mouth and utter such words as cripple, or black, or girl, and find himself out of a job.

'He likes it here,' she said. 'He can relax. The pressures aren't so great.'

'Really?' said Eve. 'I don't know much about America, but I thought you were all more relaxed out there.'

'Hah,' said Mrs Heimlich, darkly.

'Indeed?' said Eve, inquiringly.

'You have to watch your step,' said Mrs Heimlich, 'every inch of the way.'

'How tiresome,' said Eve.

'You're not kidding,' said Mrs Heimlich.

'What are you girls doing?' asked Adam, coming upon them suddenly.

'We were discussing the state of the world,' said Eve. 'If you're looking for the wine it's either in the fridge or under the sink.'

'Not for me,' said Mrs Heimlich. 'We've got to get going.' She rose from the grass and addressed her spouse. 'Harold,' she said.

'I know, honey,' he said, hastening towards her. 'We've got to get going.'

'Us too,' said the undergraduates. 'We have to go too. Come on, Ludo. We have to go now.'

'Goodbye,' said Eve, 'it was so good of you to come. It's been so pleasant.' She brushed her hair out of the eye it was hanging over and smiled mildly. It made Adam nervous, that gentle smile.

He said, 'Do you know I heard the cuckoo earlier this year, introducing himself by his own name, like Americans do at dinner parties.' Eve's smile faded. She turned back to the departing guests, none of whom seemed to have heard Adam's remark.

'Don't drink any more,' she said, out of the corner of her mouth.

'I've hardly drunk anything,' said Adam, and Eve, smiling again and waving, wondered if perhaps her husband too was going off his head.

Adam went to work on Monday morning and life began afresh for Eve. She knelt for a while in the kitchen watching the ants.

They seemed to have some definite purpose in mind, she reflected. Or maybe she only thought that because it was said that they did, that they all worked together as one, performing their different tasks. This, of course, was as nothing to the housewife whose duty it was to destroy them before they colonized the pantry shelves. She sprinkled a teaspoon of sugar on the floor and thought they paused to look up at her as though pondering her motive. Then she fed the baby on mashed banana and yoghurt and put her out in the garden under the greengage tree. She mopped the kitchen floor without looking to see whether she had drowned or discommoded any ants, for she liked to keep a clear conscience and was determined not to become overscrupulous in small matters. It did cross her mind that her impression of nothingness was erroneous and that lives as significant as her own were being played out under the kitchen sink, but she preferred not to dwell on it. The empty bottles clanked dismally as she put them in the bin liner and she separated them with newspapers and banana peel. It did seem as though life held very little. When she had made the bed she stood by the window looking down at the baby under the greengage tree, wondering what Mrs Heimlich was doing today. She envied what she thought of as Mrs Heimlich's free lifestyle, travelling around the world with no ants of her own to worry about and no baby. She had a husband, of course, but seemed hardly troubled by him. Perhaps that was something that came with age, and perhaps the prospect of nothingness became immaterial after a while.

'So what have you been doing?' inquired Adam when he returned home.

'Nothing,' said Eve.

'Any chance of supper?' asked Adam, as the silence lengthened.

'It's in the oven,' said Eve, 'but I must bath the baby first.'

'Couldn't you have done that earlier?' inquired Adam.

'No,' said Eve.

'Why not?' demanded Adam as she said no more and made no move.

Eve sighed. 'It would have been too early,' she said, getting up and reaching for the baby where it lay on the grass on a woolly blanket.

'I don't know what's the matter with you these days,' said Adam.

'I'm no different from what I ever was,' said Eve, who believed this to be so. Adam was disposed to argue but found that he couldn't remember quite wherein lay the difference. He had a sense of imbalance, a lack of tension between himself and his wife. It was as though she had drifted invisibly, impalpably closer to him, beside him, behind him so that he could no longer see her clearly and she had ceased to have reality. 'That was a good party yesterday,' he said. 'I think they all enjoyed it.' He reminded himself that Eve had made an effort, had mashed up sardines and talked to the guests. 'Shall I bath the baby?' he offered suddenly.

'Oh no,' said Eve. 'I'll do it.' She looked like a ghost in the twilight.

As she dried and powdered the baby and put her nappy on she wondered how it would be if Adam was doing it. He had on previous occasions talked to the baby in her bath, splashing her quite gently and squeezing the soap through his hands so it fell into the water, but he had never gone further than that, never picked her out all vulnerable and slippery to lie in his lap. Eve tried to picture the scene should she suddenly die without warning, insignificant as any ant, and lie on the bathroom floor lifeless and useless. What would Adam do?

*

25

'What would you do if I died,' she asked as she pushed the peas towards him. He swallowed a piece of lamb chop and bit his tongue in irritation, thinking that she was asking him if he would marry again; forget her and take another woman to wife.

'How do I know?' he said crossly. 'I suppose I'd have to marry again,' he added, thinking that he was being unkind.

'Yes,' said Eve, 'I suppose you would. Have some more peas.'

'No, thank you,' said Adam. 'They're rather dry.'

'It's because they're real ones,' said Eve. 'They're nothing like as nice as frozen ones.'

'Then why didn't you buy frozen ones?' said Adam.

'I thought these would be nicer,' said Eve. Adam put down his fork and stared at her. Somewhere in the back of his mind he remembered that she had once been more interesting than this. He had never thought her particularly witty, but surely once she had talked about things other than the rival merits of fresh or frozen peas.

'I bought them the other day,' said Eve, 'and I shelled them myself.' She had done it out of a sense of duty.

'I saw Heimlich today,' said Adam. 'We had a drink.' He racked his brain for something of interest to tell his wife, to bring her out of the shadows where he could barely discern her. 'He said his wife liked you very much.'

'He could hardly say she hated me,' observed Eve listlessly.

'He needn't have said anything,' said Adam. 'He needn't have mentioned you at all.' He tried to remember if Heimlich had indeed said anything about Eve. He was almost sure he had but they had been speaking about Hudson's article in the *TLS* and Adam had been concentrating on that. He wished he could have a similar conversation with Eve, for there were aspects he still wished to clarify in his own mind, but she wouldn't understand the issues involved. 'I wonder why fresh peas are no good,' he said. 'You'd think they would be.'

'I'd like to go to college,' said Eve. 'I'd like to study philosophy.'

'Don't be silly,' said Adam. 'You've got the baby to think about.'

'I do think about her,' said Eve, 'but I'd like to think about something else as well.' She knew what Adam would say eventually if she persisted, so she got up to move the dishes. He said it anyway.

'You haven't got that sort of mind.'

'How do you know?' asked Eve. But she knew his reasons for saying it: he himself had that sort of mind and he didn't consider there was room in a relationship for two people with the same sort of mind. 'What sort of mind do you have in mind,' she asked.

'The sort of mind that can *think*,' said Adam.

'All sorts of mind can think,' said Eve.

'Not yours,' said Adam, enraged by this arrogant perception. 'You've never had a thought in your life.'

'Well, if that's what you think,' said Eve, 'I don't think *you* can think. Not very clearly anyway.' She wondered if she would now become a victim of that domestic violence that Jones so often spoke of, for Adam was rising to his feet and his face had grown larger and red. He controlled himself with an effort and pretended he was merely leaving the table.

'Don't be silly,' he said.

'All right,' said Eve, 'but I won't live in the country any more.'

'Why do you think I said that?' Eve inquired of the baby. 'It wasn't true. I don't want to study philosophy. If I studied anything I'd rather study archaeology or dry stone walling. I'd like to study dressmaking. I don't want to do cake decorating or flower arranging, but I'd like to do something with my hands. Nothing too pretty but something clever. I'd like to make a tailored dress with inset panels. I wonder what it would look like if I sewed it all by hand with little tiny stitches. I wonder if Mrs Heimlich would be pleased with me. I expect she would if I did it well enough. If I made it from beautiful, stiff material so that it almost stood up on its own. But you wouldn't like it. It wouldn't be comfortable for a baby and if I made it too stiff I wouldn't be able to sit down in it.'

She picked up the baby and reflected on the sorrows of life, its brevity, which sometimes frightened her, and its seemingly interminable nature, which made her tired. 'We'll go and have a look at the ants,' she said to the baby. 'As there is so much nature around we might as well commune with it a bit. Look . . .' she said, crouching on the floor half under the sink. 'Look at all the little ants. They're like you, cootchy coo. Not very like you, of course, because you're prettier, but they don't think too much. I don't think you think much, do you, baby? I hope not. It would be terrible if you were thinking when I thought you were just looking.' She got up and straightened her skirt: it was made of soft cotton and fell in anarchic folds so that sometimes it was lifted by the wind, and sometimes impeded her walking. 'If I was a mandarin,' she told the baby, 'my clothes would stand up on their own. I might find them constricting, but I don't believe I should despise them.' There was an ant on her hem. 'There's one who wasn't looking where he was going,' she informed the baby. 'It's probably a girl. It's probably like me and it wants to get away and do something different. Or perhaps it knows what I'm planning and is escaping before I do it. It is my duty to wipe out this ant colony because this is Adam's house. A house built for human beings. We want no other form of life invading our territory.' She threw the ant to the floor. 'It could be a mad ant,' she said. 'An ant with learning difficulties. It might have been released into the community and the other ants have shunned it. I don't care . . .' she said. 'I am not an asylum for mad ants. I have no fellow-feeling for it.' She held the baby closely. 'Don't worry,' she reassured it. '*I'm* not at all mad. I'm not talking to myself. I'm talking to you.'

When Adam came home he found that Eve had laid the garden table for supper. There was a jug of wild flowers in the middle of it and a bee hovered winningly about the mouth of a pale antirrhinum.

'I don't know how you can suggest we should leave the country,' said Adam contentedly, sitting down on the bench and stretching his legs.

'But have you not seen the backside of the angel?' asked Eve. Adam let his glance drift slowly towards her. He said nothing and Eve went into the house, returning at once with an earthenware casserole which she placed on a wooden coaster. She lifted the lid and he smelled herbs.

'It smells delicious,' he said carefully.

'It is,' said Eve. 'It's lamb with apricots that have melted into the juice. The meat and the fruit are as one.' She spoke matter-of-factly and went back to the kitchen for a bowl of rice.

'Salad?' asked Adam.

'Green salad,' said Eve, 'with garlic and oil.'

Adam pondered this description as he ate. He wife's words, while unusual, were not ill-chosen: her account of this meal quite accurate. 'It *is* delicious,' he said.

'You never used to like fruit with meat,' said Eve.

'Your cooking's improved,' said Adam.

'The baby's asleep,' said Eve.

'I'll open a bottle of wine,' said Adam.

When she had cleared the things away Eve sat with her

hands clasped round her knees and her soft skirt looking towards the fading horizon. 'There's syllabub for pudding if you want it,' she said. 'Milk warm from the cow with lemon juice.' She was thinking of the juice of lemons and the bitterness of rejection mingled with the foolish generosity of cream – the senseless, self-sacrificial way it rose to the top of the milk, ready to be skimmed.

'What do you mean – warm from the cow?' asked Adam. 'You haven't been getting it straight from the farm, have you?' His tone was anxious and accusing.

'You can't get it straight from the farm,' said Eve. 'They won't let you. They take it all away and mess it all about in case it gives you diseases. I was using a figure of speech. They used to milk the cow into a bowl and rush back and put juice in it. Once they used to do that.'

Adam thought this over. Although not well-expressed it made a certain sense. 'Well, let's have some then,' he said. The syllabub was delicious. He finished off the bottle of wine. 'How was your day?' he asked.

Eve now considered for a while before she spoke. 'It was partly very dull,' she said, 'and partly interesting. The baby's getting more interesting, but I don't know what to do about the ants. I did a lot of cooking – but then you know that. You just ate it. I think I'm going to have to pour boiling water on the ants. I swept them up with the dustpan and brush but they came back. The way they behave is quite interesting if you watch them for long enough.'

'Then why do you want to pour boiling water on them?' asked Adam.

'Because you want to get rid of them,' said Eve.

'Don't blame me for your sadistic tendencies,' said Adam, and Eve went early to bed.

Adam sat up quite late wondering what his wife had meant

by her remark about the backside of the angel. Perhaps she'd been quoting some obscure poem from some anthology of inferior verse. He hoped that she had. In the kitchen he noticed that she had left dishes and pans unwashed. He bent down and looked under the sink to see if there was any sign of ants, and seeing none rolled up his sleeves, filled the basin with hot water and slowly washed up all the dishes. He moved his feet hardly at all and then very carefully for fear of treading on Eve's ants.

The morning dawned fine. Adam hummed as he got dressed. Eve, lying on her side with a corner of the sheet in her mouth, wondered what the sound was: she had never heard a man humming before. She had never heard one singing on a private occasion, not even in the bath as they were reported to do. When they were first married Eve had often hummed, especially first thing in the morning, but Adam had bidden her be silent, telling her it was an irritating habit. It was, realized Eve as she went into the kitchen. It was intensely irritating.

'What time will you be home?' she asked, to make him talk so that he would have to cease humming.

'What time would you like me to be home?' asked Adam, thinking that she must be planning a supper dish of such refinement that it required delicate timing and prompt attention.

But Eve said she didn't care what time he was home; not in an unfriendly or even impolite manner, but as one who respects the freedom of another to go his own way and make his own decisions about when he wishes to eat his supper.

Adam found it strangely frightening. There are cold and lonely aspects of freedom.

'I washed the dishes,' he said.

'Thank you,' said Eve, who was waiting for him to go so

that she could wash them again properly. They were covered in a thin film of garlic-flavoured grease.

'I thought I'd ask some people for a drink on Sunday,' said Adam.

'If you do I'll kill myself,' said Eve.

'Don't be silly,' said Adam.

'I will,' said Eve. 'I will.'

'I'll help you,' said Adam, and went on to say that he would assist in tidying up and would do the shopping if she would just give him a list of what she wanted.

'Hemlock,' said Eve.

'I'll ask the Heimlichs,' said Adam.

When he had gone she stood in silence, but it was too quiet. 'There is intelligent life under that sink,' she said aloud.

Adam and Professor Heimlich had lunch together in the pub. Adam said, 'I'm worried about Eve.' Professor Heimlich said, 'Don't worry. Would you like another pint?' and Adam had another pint and the other half of the professor's sandwich, for Professor Heimlich was watching his weight. As he spoke Adam had realized that it was out of character for him to talk about his wife: it indicated, he thought, a previously concealed sensitivity in his personality, a maturity that he had not before been required to make evident. Perhaps almost a feminine side; something gentle and compassionate that had lain dormant until called upon. 'She seems a bit low,' he said.

'Maybe she spends too much time on her own,' said the professor, glancing round to see if any other of his colleagues were lunching in this rather unappealing pub.

'She's not gregarious,' said Adam. 'She likes being on her own. She potters round the garden.'

If this was the case the professor couldn't see what the problem was. 'Women are tougher than you think,' he observed.

Relieved, Adam agreed that this was probably so.

She washed the dishes and she washed the baby and she washed the clothes. She washed her T-shirt and her cotton skirt and left them lying on the draining-board. Nothing – she thought. Now there's nothing to do. She went into the garden and back into the house, and then into the garden again. She looked at the pansies and they beamed back at her. They don't mean it, she thought. They reminded her of the university women, some of whom were ardent feminists who tended to cluster like pansies, beaming. She had never noticed before how smug and self-righteous a pansy could look. She wondered what the torturer was doing at this moment and what God thought about it all.

'I'm going to sing you a song, baby,' she said and lifted up her voice. 'I'm a little prairie flower, growing wilder every hour. Nobody can cultivate me. Whoops, I'm a pansy.' She became aware of the tractor in the field. 'Where there is a tractor in this vicinity,' she said under her breath, 'there will undoubtedly also be a Jones. We must take evasive action,' and she went back into the house, clutching her baby tightly. She knelt down and put the baby on a rug. 'If I get under the sink,' she said, 'then if Jones comes begging for tea and cake he won't see me. And if he does, if he has the cheek to walk in and find me, I'll just say I was sorting out the ants.'

After a while came the voice, 'You there?' called Jones. 'Anybody home?' Eve stayed quite still, her finger to her lips. Even when he'd gone she still crouched on the cold floor feeling closer to the ants.

'The noonday devil,' she said, 'is worse than the business that stalketh about in the dark, even more frightening than whoever it is who comes to walk in the garden in the cool of the evening.'

33

How glad I am she thought, that I didn't say that to Adam, for he wouldn't have understood. She reflected that she could have said it to Mrs Heimlich, who would probably have thought her imaginative, whereas Adam would have considered her crazy. But better on the whole – she decided – just to say it to myself.

Jones, in his turn, went to lunch in the pub. 'Barmy,' he told his friends. 'Mad. One minute she's singing her head off in the garden and the next she's sat under the sink with her head in her hands. I saw her through the window and I yelled through the door and she took not a blind bit of notice.' He was aggrieved, having thought her friendly.

'Probably her time of the month,' said his friends.

'Yeah,' agreed Jones.

'Because,' said Eve earnestly to Mrs Heimlich, 'sometimes the garden seems less like a garden than a charnel house.' She was trying to make herself clear. 'The flowers don't live very long and then they die and I see it all the time. I see winter coming, and then when it's spring those silly flowers think it's time to come out again.'

'It's the progression of the seasons,' said Mrs Heimlich. 'It's inspired poets through the ages. You should write.'

'It's the earth,' said Eve. 'Things come out of the earth and then they go back into it and what, you wonder, what on earth is the point?' She looked fearfully to where the baby lay, separated from the terrible earth by a woolly blanket.

'You may still be suffering,' said Mrs Heimlich, 'from post-parturition melancholy. Nobody ever takes it sufficiently seriously.'

'If I am,' said Eve, 'I think I've always had it. Ever since I was born myself. Perhaps everyone everywhere suffers from it always.'

The drinks party was similar to the last one, the same people present with the exception of Ludo, who, it seemed, was particularly confused at the moment. There was another difference: Adam had tied a tea towel about his waist and had made ham sandwiches. Occasionally he hummed.

'He's taken over the catering,' said Eve. 'God knows what's got into him. He says he wants to help but he's a nuisance. His ham sandwiches are horrible.'

'And we're Jewish,' said Mrs Heimlich. Adding, 'Womb envy.'

'Pardon?' said Eve.

'He's trying to prove he can do whatever you can do,' explained Mrs Heimlich. 'He envies your womb.'

'He's welcome to it,' said Eve.

'No, he's not,' said Mrs Heimlich. 'It makes you appear redundant.'

'I thought that was what women were supposed to do to men,' said Eve.

'It works both ways,' said Mrs Heimlich, 'in the battle of the sexes.'

'Another sandwich?' Adam offered.

'Thank you, no,' said Mrs Heimlich.

'I want to live in a city,' said Eve. She thought this sounded a little bald and rephrased it. 'How I long to go back to the city.' She looked towards the opening of the path that led away from the garden. 'He won't let me,' she said.

Mrs Heimlich naturally assumed she was speaking of her husband, being unaware that Eve descried a dim yet implacable form poised not to exclude but to imprison her. 'You tell him,' she advised.

'I sometimes think he's the foul fiend,' said Eve, and shivered, for images of the vile god Pan assailed her in the summer's heat.

35

'We all think that sometimes,' said Mrs Heimlich reassuringly.

The professor strolled over to them. 'The boys seem to think Ludo's not long for this world,' he remarked.

'Lucky him,' said Eve.

'You mustn't talk like that,' said the professor. 'Here you are in this little earthly paradise . . .'

Eve screamed.

The Heimlichs sat side by side in bed. 'Adam said he was worried about her,' observed the professor, 'only the other day.'

Mrs Heimlich said nothing.

'I never imagined things were as bad as that,' he went on. 'Poor Adam.' Mrs Heimlich lay down and gazed at the ceiling.

THE CAT'S WHISKERS

She woke early, as she always did now. It was one of the signs of age, she told herself. It could not be long before there would be plenty of time to sleep.

'Oh for God's sake,' she said aloud, smiling insincerely at the morning air. Her awareness of the prospect of death depressed her not so much because of its inevitability as because it made her wonder if she was falling prey to self-pity, losing her sense of humour. That would be intolerable. 'When I go,' she said to the cat, 'I will go with all guns blazing. Death will not take me prisoner without a fight.'

I'm glad I only said that to the cat, she thought. What a boring remark. The cat requested its breakfast. Sensible beast. She asked whether it had slept well. It patted her ankle with its paw, not over-demandingly but confidently expectant. 'Such a clever cat,' she said to it.

'Damn cat,' said her husband walking into the kitchen. He had elected himself the cat's enemy, perhaps out of some obscure sense of structure: his wife loved the cat therefore he would not. It made everything neater somehow, more balanced. She turned on the radio and hummed as best she could to the strains of an unfamiliar tune.

'Where's my gun?' he inquired. She had forgotten he was going shooting and her spirits rose. Today would be her own and she would walk in the garden and later sit in the comfortable armchair. She might even watch the dreadful morning television.

'Where you left it, ducky,' she said, wondering as she always did why he asked such odd questions. He frowned at the jug of roses on the table.

'Those are Elizabeth of Glamis,' he said. 'I've told you I wish you wouldn't pick those. Let's have some quiet,' and he turned off the radio. She contemplated turning it on again but he had gone to the bathroom and there would have been no point. She disliked modern music as much as he did.

'I wonder why Elizabeth is sacrosanct,' she mused. 'She grows like a weed.' Her husband's voice came down the stairs, muffled by the sound of running water.

'The water's cold,' he told her. 'Did you see to the boiler?' She straightened up and put her hand to the small of her back, arching it slightly, like a person in a film expressing physical weariness. He didn't really expect an answer.

'No,' she mouthed silently, 'I didn't see to the boiler. Did you see to the boiler, cat? He always sees to the boiler. Why should he suppose I've suddenly taken it into my head to see to the boiler?' She made another gesture more usual on the stage than in real life, holding her head with both hands and rolling her eyes upwards. Such silent, unseen manifestations of unease, of her sense of oppression had become habitual with her. She had become an actress in her own life. As good a way to survive as any.

'Will you ring the boiler people,' he called, 'and fix me a bacon sandwich? I don't want to be late.'

'That would be a shame,' she said. 'All those pheasants got up early, you wouldn't want to keep them waiting.' She hummed under her breath as the bacon began to sizzle.

'Where's my breakfast?' he asked, looking at the frying-pan as he crossed the kitchen.

'It's here, my darling,' she said, and out of old habit she added, 'and for goodness' sake dry your hair or you'll get pneumonia . . .' People who have brought up children find it difficult not to make this sort of remark, sometimes even to strangers.

'I've found it,' he said, fondling his gun.

'Well don't point it at me,' said his wife, suddenly pettish. 'I'm not a pheasant. I hate pheasants. They have very small eyes.'

'Fine example of workmanship, this gun,' he observed, peering down the barrels. He sounded defensive, as though she had called him infantile. 'Pow, pow,' he said. 'This for me?' he asked, reaching for the sandwich.

'It was going to be for the Empress of China,' said his wife, and felt briefly ashamed for taking an unfair advantage of his weakness, 'but you're welcome. And for goodness' sake, go and get dressed.'

He went obediently, carrying the sandwich and she knew that if she had told him to sit down and eat it nicely he would have done so. She picked up the gun and said, 'Pow, pow,' handling it curiously. 'I've never liked these things,' she said. 'This is the bit you pull, cat. See? Then it goes bang, and some mother's child is all ruined and spoiled and dead. Blown to bits. Bang.'

'Where the hell are my socks?' inquired her husband from above, where he was out of sight, away from her disconcerting glance.

'Try the drawer,' she shouted. 'Do I ask him where my socks are?' she demanded of the cat. 'What would he say if I asked him where my socks were? Darling,' she whispered, wiping out the frying-pan, 'where is my chiffon blouse? The one with the embroidery and the tasselled fringe? Where are my golden gloves, and the beaded sash my father gave me?'

'Why don't you change your mind and come too,' called her husband, who was pulling on a sock at the time. 'Jane is going and Jenny. You like Jenny . . .'

'I've got too much to do here,' she called back. 'I'm too busy.'

'What have you got to do?' demanded her husband boldly. 'You've got a cleaner, haven't you?'

'She's off sick,' yelled his wife, adding, for her own satisfaction, 'she discovered a bubo under her armpit.'

'A what?' he cried.

'Nothing, just nothing at all.'

'What did you say?' He went to the top of the stairs and looked down, straining his ears to hear her.

'I said I had to sort out the linen cupboard,' she said rapidly. 'And polish the spoons and pick the caterpillars off the cabbage and write a letter to your aunt in Australia.'

'What?' He could hear only a muttering and wondered worriedly if he was really going deaf. Such hints of age depressed him.

'Nothing,' she said clearly.

Relieved that he had heard this he buttoned his shirt. 'You're silly,' he said. 'You don't know what you're missing.'

'Oh, I know what I'm missing,' she said, scratching the cat behind its ears. 'I'm missing sitting in a car all day, creeping along the lanes with the women while the men go bounding around in the undergrowth, popping off at those wretched birds. Why does he say I like Jenny? I can't stand Jenny. She wears her waxed jacket to bed and she's losing her hair. I have always been moderately civil to Jenny. I suppose that could be construed as liking – but then I'm moderately civil to every-body. Perhaps he thinks I like everybody. I don't, cat. I don't like everybody at all.' She ran her hand along its back to indicate that however sour she had become she excepted cats from her disapproval.

'Have you seen my club tie?' came a cry.

'No,' she enunciated. 'Of course I've seen his club tie,' she said to her furry friend. 'I've seen it more times than I care to remember – round his neck, hanging over the back of the chair, lying on the floor. I was with him when he bought it. Cat, do you remember the old days before you were spayed? Do you remember those nights in the garden, waving your tail at the gentlemen? Wondering where they were? No? Perhaps it's just as well. I don't really remember the past either.' She sighed. 'I tell a lie. I remember – oh, so long ago – I remember sitting by the telephone and waiting for it to ring. And do you know whose voice I was waiting for?'

'You must have seen it,' cried her husband, his voice plaintive.

'That's it,' she said. 'That's the voice I was waiting for.'

'It's in the tie press on the right of the wardrobe,' she shouted. 'Unless, of course, he's tied up Elizabeth of Glamis with it in an idle moment.' She stopped stroking the cat and stared out of the window, waiting.

'It isn't here,' he cried again.

'Yes it is,' she said calmly. 'Wait for it, cat.'

'No it . . . Oh, yes all right, I see.'

She turned on the sink tap. 'There . . . Mind you, cat, to be fair, I sometimes do the same thing. Many's the time I've gone looking for the mustard and I can't see it. I'm looking straight at it but I can't see it. I wonder why that is? Some would say I don't want to see it, and I must admit making mustard is boring. Perhaps he's bored with his tie. Sometimes I look straight at him and I don't really see him. Do you know what the greatest release in the world is, cat? It's the release from love. Well, they call it love.'

She turned the tap off and wondered where the terror arose: the quick terror that came on her unexpectedly, fracturing the light so that she didn't know where to look, disorienting, horrible. Something she couldn't describe, even to the cat, even to herself, for despite its intensity it seemed too trivial to mention.

'When that woman comes you might get her to do something about the state of this wardrobe,' said her husband from the security of the bedroom.

'Why, my darling?' she asked sweetly, almost relieved to raise her voice, to pretend that at one and the same time she had found a focus for her fear and a way of denying it.

'Because it's in a hell of a mess,' he said in reasonable tones.

'Well, of course it is,' she said, almost light-hearted again. 'He's gone through it like a badger. You were so wise, cat, in your unregenerate days, only to meet your mate in the moon shadow, in the gloaming – a little passion, some howling, howling – then, whoosh, you came back to the kitchen to have your kittens; nice little furry, furry kittens; and your mate went loping off. God knows where he went. Did you know, cat? No, of course you didn't. What did you care? You had your babies and your basket and four walls around you. Did you notice that uncastrated tomcats never laugh? They have that air of urgency, as though they felt here was something enormously important they had to do. Did you ever notice that?'

She felt as though she had made a discovery, had contrived to impose some order on, some explanation for, the chaos that threatened her. She went on speaking half under her breath, hurriedly. 'They look very serious and rather worried because they have to impregnate all those females and fight all the males. Serious stuff. No laughing matter. They have to live alone. No one could put up with them in the house – all that sorrowful, pressing importance, the smell, the clawing. You wouldn't want him around much, would you, cat?'

'I still wish you'd come,' called the man upstairs. A different man now: conciliatory, a little plaintive.

Her courage strengthened. The dancing demons, the imps of insecurity receded. After all, her unease was only the human condition. She almost felt as though she could laugh. 'I bet your mate never said that to you, did he, Grimalkin?' she suggested to the cat. 'He didn't want you around. Your tribe hasn't progressed like ours has. You meat eaters. You haven't changed since the – oh, since the ancient Egyptians made gods of you. Now *we* are different. Once upon a time our men – toms to you, cat – would take up their clubs and their bows and arrows and go hunting, but not for little mice. They went out chasing big, hairy, dangerous things with horns and hooves.'

She raised her arms above her head to demonstrate the fearful hugeness of the horns; she widened her eyes to show the awful incomprehension of the hunted beasts. 'Big, fat animals,' she said; 'full of cholesterol and probably infested with parasites. Savage, terrified, dangerous things. Do you see the fun in chasing them? Now the women – queans to you, cat – didn't do that. They stayed put round the cave mouth – I'm afraid to tell you, cat, we lived in holes like mice. Or so they say – but don't let that prejudice you – and they ate the nuts and berries that they picked off the trees and bushes, and they gossiped away among themselves and agreed what fools men were – risking their lives chasing big fat animals – and they laughed a lot. Like this . . .' And now she felt that she could laugh, and she did.

'Darling . . .?'

She stopped and uttered a little moan. 'Yes.'

'What are you doing.'

'Nothing.'

'What are you laughing at?'

'Just something I heard on the radio,' she said half in defiance, half in resignation.

'The radio isn't on,' he said sternly.

'Oh, isn't it?' she said.

'You're spending too much time on your own,' her husband explained from above. 'You're going mad.'

'They always say that, cat,' she said. 'When they can't understand you, they tell you you're going mad. I used to believe him – a long, long time ago. When he was angry I trembled. I used to iron his handkerchiefs. That was before I remembered Kleenex. I used to think that he must be right about everything. Just as those women in their caves might have thought it was clever of the men to go and get gored and trampled chasing hamburgers. He went to the office every day and I stayed at home with the children, and every morning before he left he would say, "What are you going to do today, darling?" And every evening when he came home he'd say, "What have you done today, darling?" And I'd say, "Oh, nothing, darling."' She shuddered and began to wash the dishes with naked hands in the hot water. Too late to worry about the skin of her hands. Her fear had changed to regret, for the children were grown up and gone. 'Because I'd only cooked and cleaned and fed the baby,' she continued determinedly. 'And washed the clothes and the children, and sung them songs and pushed them on the swing. Not a lot. You see that's the sort of thing women do, and whatever women do, it isn't work. Not *work*. What men do is work, you see, cat. Even if it's only shooting birds.' She was surprised and annoyed to feel tears in her eyes but there was nothing she could do about it for her hands were covered in detergent.

'Hell, I'm going to be late,' said the father of her children. 'Have you got my lunch ready?'

'Nearly ready, darling,' she lied. She wiped her hands on her dressing-gown and went to the fridge, staring at the contents, wondering what she was doing. There was pâté, there was smoked salmon and for a moment she forgot what it was usual to do with these things. Sandwiches, she reminded herself. You wrap them up in bread. She'd done it so often her memory had failed her out of sheer weariness. Making sandwiches was probably the most boring task the housewife could perform.

'Do you want a boiled egg?' she called. Boiling eggs seemed rather more creative. The water moved around at least.

'You forgot to put the salt in last time,' said her husband. 'Tyler said eating a boiled egg without salt was like kissing a woman with a moustache.' He laughed.

'Goodness, how droll,' said his wife.

'What?'

'Nothing.'

'You've started talking to yourself a lot.' He moved again to the top of the stairs and gazed down although he couldn't see her.

'Once upon a time, cat,' she said under her breath, 'when the men were in pursuit of the hairy rhinoceros, I should've had the women of the tribe to talk to. But they've been corrupted by civilization, taken in by what their mates say. They're all sitting in cars following the chase. Now do you think the cave woman would have wasted her time sitting around on the savannah in a Range Rover? No, of course she wouldn't. Far too much sense.' She watched the water beginning to move and the eggs trying helplessly to get out. Quickly she started whispering again. 'Now you may say, cat, you may want to point out to me that my cave woman also benefited from the slaughter of these animals. Fur coats, you might say to me – although considering your own species it is a delicate matter and perhaps you prefer not to dwell on it – but if you put aside your natural reservations, you just might want to remind me that the skins kept the women warm too. And to this I would answer that if man had left the beasts alone, woman would – with her native ingenuity, which has been suppressed by circumstance and the jealous envy of men – she, as I say, would have invented fake fur long before the animal-rights protestors started fussing about it. And meat? Protein? Remember the nuts. Nuts are simply humming with protein. And remember how all over the Western world men are eating T-bone steaks and dropping dead from heart attacks.'

She emptied away the boiling water and ran the cold tap over the eggs, raising her voice. 'Now, if they'd followed the example of the women and stuck to nuts they'd never have got this problem. The women, you see, never got to eat much meat in the cave – the odd ear or knuckle-bone – because the men needed it all so they could conserve their energy to go and catch more meat. I hope I'm not offending you, cat, with this dismissive talk of meat. I quite understand that it is all that agrees with your digestive system. *Homo sapiens* is different. You can tell by our teeth.' She bent, and by way of demonstration, snarled at the cat. 'See? Omnivorous, we are. That is, we can eat almost anything – from pieces of big dangerous animals, right down through nuts and winnowed grasses to blancmange. I have to confess, cat, I've never fancied mice. The Romans used to eat dormice, but they were given to what became known with the rise of civilization as *luxuria* . . .' She had turned off the tap but forgotten to lower her voice.

'What did you say?' came the query.

'I said the Romans ate mice.'

'Why did you say that? Who are you talking to?'

'The cat,' she said defiantly.

There was a short silence. 'You *are* going mad,' he said, and she thought he sounded resigned but triumphant.

'He is incorrect, you know, cat,' she said, defiance increasing. 'Once I was going mad. Once I was giving dinner parties twice a week and going to them three times a week. Now that's mad if you like. Always the same people and the same food. Marinated kipper fillets I remember were all the rage at one time, and grilled grapefruits. And the men used to talk about the wine, and I may be doing them an injustice but, to the best of my recollection, the women used to talk about the whiteness of their wash. Now, there's an interesting thing, cat. Perhaps the poor creatures were expressing an atavistic nostalgia for the days when the women gathered at the river and trampled on the clothes and battered them with flat stones and talked and talked to each other. The men put a stop to that. They invented washing-machines. They had to break up the women, you see. They were frightened of what they were saying. They feared a plot and also, cat, they knew damn well that what the women were saying about *them* would not give them comfort to hear. They could hear them laughing down by the river.'

'I may bring a couple of chaps back for a bite of supper,' said her husband in the casual tone of a man doing up his tie.

She stopped in the middle of cracking an egg and lifted her head. 'Don't do that,' she said reprovingly as though he had made a childish but improper suggestion.

'What?'

'I said there isn't any supper. I'm defrosting the freezer and all there is is a tiny cauliflower cheese and a Cornish pasty.'

'Can't you do some spaghetti or soup or something?' he inquired. He sounded polite but there was something wrong with the way he phrased himself.

'I'm not a magician you know,' she retorted, shouting. Her voice fell. 'What I am is a liar. I have a great deal of delicious food, and not one morsel is going down the gullet of Tyler. Not a scrap. Tyler's missus would feed them. Tyler's missus is a perfect example of a woman driven mad by the men. She does what he tells her, and she's stuffed so full of Valium she doesn't even rattle any more. Do you know what she does? She tells people what Tyler says. She says, "My husband always says ..." or "Jim says ..." or "That's what Jim thinks" or "Jim doesn't think that." It's enough to make a cat laugh. What do you think, cat? Funny, huh? What's more she's called Edith. Poor thing. Perhaps much should be forgiven a person called Edith. I don't know whether you've noticed, cat, but the woman I am now is light years away from the woman I was then in her Laura Ashley frock ...' There was an old mirror on the wall. She moved and looked into it.

'Then we'll probably go back to Tyler's place,' he said as one who against his better nature must needs disappoint.

'OK,' she said.

'What?'

'I said that's a good idea,' she yelled.

'If I was Tyler's missus I would take his gun and blow his head off, but she will take lemons and scoop them out and fill them with mackerel mousse and set them before him and his friends, and she will have freshly ironed napkins, and warmed plates for their goulash, and chilled plates for their ice-cream. It makes me think of butter in a lordly dish. That's what it makes me think of, cat. Jael and Sisera – she banged a nail in his head after tea. Actually I have been less than frank with you. I know when I came to my senses. It was when his father died. I thought then – one day it will be him and I will be glad. Now that's not a nice thing to think of the person with whom you have shared bed and board for many years. Not nice at all. It gave me a nasty shock. Good little women in their Laura Ashley frocks don't think like that. That's when I gave away my Laura Ashley frock to Oxfam. I have to live with myself, you see. Not just with him, but with myself. Somehow there was one too many of us so the frock had to go.'

'Is my lunch ready? Don't forget the salt,' he instructed her.

'I tried to cut down his salt because it's bad for his blood pressure,' she told the cat. 'Where is it?' She buttered the bread and started slicing the pâté. The cat spoke in the way of a cat who still hasn't had her breakfast. 'Oh cat, I'm sorry,' said the woman. 'I was so interested in our discussion I forgot your breakfast. I must be getting absent-minded.' She cut off a sliver of pâté and held it out between her finger and thumb. The cat ate it, licked the woman's finger and thumb and its own chin, and asked for more. 'Hang on,' she said, 'where's your tin? What have we today? Ah – "Carefully chosen meaty chunks in a rich gravy with chicken morsels added." I wonder what that means. They probably dug up some old bison,' she said and paused in opening the tin for the thought of absent-mindedness had given her an idea. She put the pâté on a plate and the plate on the floor. 'Take that,' she said to the cat. She emptied the tin of cat food into a basin and began mashing it up with a fork, breaking up its carefully chosen meaty chunks. It smelled savoury. She drained away some of its rich gravy down the sink, wondering precisely which morsels of chicken had gone into its composition. Then she spread it on the bread and closed the sandwiches. After a moment she opened them again and sprinkled them with salt. 'Now,' she said to the cat, 'I will put them in this useful, hygienic plastic box with the patent seal for the ever-fresh effect and I will arrange some watercress on them as a garnish. Such garnish . . .', she told the cat, 'always reminds me of wreaths, of what are known as floral tributes, an attempt to conceal the fact that here in these tender morsels we have mortality.'

'Still talking to yourself,' observed her husband in quite a friendly way as he entered the kitchen, smelling pleasantly of soap and toothpaste.

'Here's your lunch and here's your gun,' she said handing it to him carefully by the barrel.

'Careful,' he said. 'So what are you going to do today, darling?'

'Oh, nothing, darling,' she said. 'Have you got your scarf? And make sure Tyler tries these sandwiches. They're special.'

When he'd gone she turned on the radio again. 'I know what's going to happen next,' she said to the cat against the noise of modern music. 'After all that pâté you're going to be sick.' She knelt and kissed the cat between the ears by way of apology.

THE FIRE IN THE ATTIC

It was a big house, big enough for the children to have the attic floor completely to themselves, but Rachel at fourteen considered that she had outgrown the playroom and seldom went up there. She had a stereo in her bedroom and practised dance steps and looking beautiful. Sometimes the mirror which she relied on for reassurance would show that she had a spot on her chin and this would preoccupy her for days until it went away. She was at a preoccupied age. So was Emily. Emily was six and, instead of dreaming and planning to become a princess, she thought she was one. When she wasn't being a princess she was most usually being a mother. Sometimes she had a flying carpet, and quite often she was in the army driving tanks, helping her father run the family zoo. (Her real father was in insurance, only Emily was too young to know or care about that.) But for a large part of the time she was concerned with her children. She would say to Rachel: 'Rachel, Rachel, if a mother is eighteen can she be in the paratroopers and have a child of two and a toddler of eighteen months and work in a shop in the evenings? Could she be a pop singer too, and a dancer, and could a mother who was eighteen have a child of nine?' Rachel, from the depths of her preoccupation, would sometimes say: 'Mmm, yes,' and Emily would persist: 'Rachel, Rachel, are you sure? Rachel, you're not listening to me. Raaachel!' Then Rachel would get cross because she was engrossed with the problem of how to bring herself to the attention of her currently most favoured pop star, or how she could contrive to keep Prince Edward unmarried until she was old enough to marry him herself. Then she would say: 'No, of course not, silly. You're so thick,' and Emily would go back to the playroom trying vainly to do sums in her head about the ages of her progeny, but not really minding too much. Everything was possible up in the attic.

Their mother was preoccupied as well. She had a friend called James and it would have been difficult to decide who disliked him more, the children or their father. Emily was silent in his presence and Rachel was overtly rude to him as only a girl of her age could afford to be. She was too old to smack, yet – as even her mother despairingly conceded – too young to know better. Their father called him 'old man' and poured him large drinks and left the room as soon as he decently could. James had the sort of job that left him a lot of free time and he took their mother shopping in the town. She said she was afraid of driving in the country lanes since the local farmer's tractor had nearly forced her Volvo into the ditch. She always came home smiling and full of gaiety but she always came home before nightfall, the adulterer's hour, so there was really nothing anyone could say. It is entirely possible that no one even considered the question of adultery. Emily certainly didn't. They just couldn't stand James. He was, himself, clearly so fond and proud of James that even if he had not been loud and vulgar there would have been little room for the esteem of others.

He used to give them all presents with the unspoken assumption that they had neither the money nor the wit to buy such things for themselves. For their mother he bought a telephone in the form of Mickey Mouse. It looked out of place in the drawing-room where she had put it but she professed to find it charming. For their father he bought a golfing umbrella which their father put in the broom cupboard. For Rachel he bought a black negligée. She tried it on once in the shamefaced half-expectation that it might make her look more princess-like. It didn't. Rachel was old enough to know what it did make her look like and she threw it away in the bin. Rather to her surprise her mother never questioned her about it. Her mother was at the age when masculine attention was unprecedentedly welcome but she wasn't stupid. The children didn't know whether she was stupid or not. They only knew she was their mother and they didn't like James. James gave Emily a teddy bear.

One day a spot appeared on Rachel's nose. It was a terrible spot, simply enormous. To Rachel it seemed bigger than her nose. She locked herself in her bedroom and dabbed it with antiseptic. She daubed it with make-up foundation. She forbade herself to squeeze it. It became the focus, the very centre of her life. Her mother said: 'Oh darling, don't worry about it. It's your age.' She said: 'James is driving me to the supermarket.' She put on her coat and said: 'Now darling, I *can* trust you to keep an eye on Emily, can't I? She's playing in the attic and she won't be any trouble at all.' She didn't wait for an answer but went out of the front door, smelling of flowers.

James had arrived early that morning and carried in a pile of logs from the woodshed. Then he had helped himself to half a Melton Mowbray pie in the fridge and sat down in their father's chair at the kitchen table. Rachel had said to him: 'You think you're our father, and you're *not*.' She had sneered at him from under her red and swollen nose which was making her even ruder than usual. She had said 'Prat,' very loudly as she left the kitchen. Her mother had laughed in a forced kind of way and James had laughed in a mirthless kind of way. He had reached out to Emily, who was resisting a babyish impulse to cling to her mother's skirt, and said:

'*You're* my little sweetheart, aren't you?' and Emily had skipped swiftly out of his grip – so swiftly that he nearly fell from his chair. James had laughed again and Emily hadn't at all liked the sound, or the expression on his face.

She felt lonely as she watched her mother being driven away and she wanted to cry. 'Rachel,' she said to her sister, 'could a lady of twenty have twins . . .'

'Oh shut up, you silly brat,' said Rachel, locking herself in her room with her nose and putting on her stereo.

Emily was deeply offended. She no longer wanted to cry. It was time to do something independent and show her relations that she was a person of some importance in her own right. For a long time now she had been considering the possibility of giving her dolls a birthday party with a cake and candles, but she knew no one would let her unless an adult was present to strike the match, and everyone was too busy with their noses and their Jameses. Even her father was tired and short-tempered when he came home. Once upon a time, he had read stories to her and played wild animals, but now he barely spoke to her except when they went away on holidays.

She went into the kitchen and got a cup-cake out of a packet in the cake tin. She got the candles out of the drawer where they lay with the paper napkins and coloured straws for parties. She got the matches from the shelf by the gas stove.

Her favourite doll was called Sellotape and cried real tears. Her father had bought it for her for her third birthday and, when everyone howled with laughter and said you couldn't call a doll Sellotape, said that he thought it a delightful name. The other most important children were a rag doll called Alexandra, a grown-up doll called Amy, a pink stuffed kitten called Kitten and a Welsh doll in a cape and hat called Gwyneth. Then there was the bear. The bear wasn't called anything. He had a mouth made of black wool turned down in a perpetual snarl, and, while once a device in his stomach had played 'The Teddy Bears' Picnic', now it was broken and silent. Emily felt towards him the mixture of guilt and dislike that many adults feel towards stepchildren; nevertheless, like many adults, she could not bring herself in all conscience to exclude him from the birthday party. She propped the children round the small chairs and lit the candles – with three matches in the end because she was so afraid of burning her fingers as the little flame crept down the wood towards them. The matches dropped on the polished boards and she put her foot on them very quickly. From downstairs came the strains of Madonna singing 'True Blue', so Rachel was still closeted with her spotted nose. All the same, Emily thought it would be sensible to lock the playroom door. The key was only used when they went away, to keep burglars from taking the synthesizer, the computer, the TV and the video equipment. Besides, Rachel was always locking her door. She climbed on a chair to get the key from the hook in the passage and, after some difficulty, succeeded in turning it in the lock.

When she looked round, the bear had fallen forward and was lying with his nose in the cake. Flames had consumed his whiskers and were curling round his ears. The paper tablecloth was burning fiercely and a plastic mug was slowly melting. Emily didn't scream because Rachel was listening to Madonna and her mother was out, and there wouldn't have been any point. She picked up Sellotape and went to unlock the door. After a while she realized that she couldn't unlock it. She really couldn't. So she went to the window past the table, which was itself beginning to blaze. Her mother was home – getting out of the car. Emily screamed then and banged on the window. She couldn't open it because it was screwed down at the bottom. Her mother looked up and saw her, and Emily waved her arms, and her mother waved back. Emily thought that this was a case where no one would mind if she broke the window, so she banged and banged on it but it wouldn't break. It was Sellotape who broke the window. Emily was never quite sure how it happened since she was certain that she would never have used her favourite child as a hammer, but there is no doubt that the window shattered and the head and shoulders of Sellotape appeared in the open air, hanging on the shards of glass. Then Emily's mother screamed too and raced into the house and up the stairs, James following. It was James who had to break the door down and stamp on the flames. He bruised his shoulder and scorched his ankles but Emily's mother didn't seem to care. Emily's mother was white with fear and anger and relief and another emotion which Emily might have recognized if she'd thought about it since she was feeling guilty herself. The dolls were mostly unharmed, except for the bear, which was smouldering and emitting noxious fumes and smiling. Emily noticed this without undue surprise, as she had always suspected he was a bad bear. His woollen mouth was turned up instead of down.

'James,' said her mother, ordering him about in a rather different tone from usual, 'take all the burned things including that bear and get rid of them.' The broken device in the bear's stomach reactivated itself: 'If you go down in the woods today . . .' sang the bear's belly.

'Get rid of it *now*,' said Emily's mother in a rising voice, and James went. Oddly enough he never came back. The last they heard of him was '. . . you're sure of a big surprise' as he receded down the drive with his smouldering bear.

The spot on Rachel's nose went away the next day and she emerged from her preoccupations long enough to be polite and quite kind to Emily. Her mother never left her unattended again until she was sixteen, and her father played wild animals with her that night. Emily grew up very happily, but until the day she died she had a faintly uneasy feeling that justice had not been properly done. *Somebody* should have smacked her for lighting those candles.

OH, BILLY

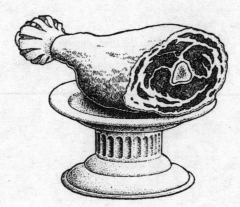

Bea was the last to arrive at the house. The undertaker was there already, sitting, all in black, in the hearse, with the coffin half-hidden under flowers.

Mother wasn't as pleased to see Bea as she usually was, because now she was here they were ready to go and Billy wouldn't be coming back. She'd prepared his favourite tea, and she kept wondering why, since he wasn't going to enjoy it. She'd been very particular with the butcher about the precise piece of ham she wanted, making him stick a skewer right down to the bone so that she could sniff it for any hint of corruption. The butcher had been quite annoyed. It was years since she'd done that, and it wasn't really necessary these days now that they had refrigeration and it was all so hygienic, but she'd wanted everything to be perfect for Billy's tea, although she knew he wouldn't be having any. It seemed so absurd that she couldn't help smiling as they went down the path, wondering what they ate in Heaven. Billy would have something to say if it didn't come up to scratch. He'd take on all the Heavenly Hosts if his bacon wasn't crispy and his egg wasn't flipped over for just a second after the gas was turned off. Her smile broadened under her dark pink hat – dark aster-pink was Billy's favourite colour. He abominated black.

Her sister-in-law observed her smiling and nudged her husband as they reached the gate. She'd never had much time for Billy's wife, who had always been too ready for a laugh, but it was a bit off, grinning like that with her husband's corpse lying ahead of her in the road – in a manner of speaking. All that business in the butcher's too. Most women who'd just been widowed wouldn't be bothering with the colour of the ham and the depth of the fat.

She'd always said their Billy was a fool. Anyone could get round him.

She indicated to some mucky-looking children sitting on the wall that they should go away. 'Scram,' she said. 'Can't you see there's been a death?'

'They come to Dad for stories,' said Bea, speaking coldly, as she couldn't stand her aunt.

The four of them, Mother and Bea and Billy's sister and brother-in-law got into the black car behind the hearse, and everyone else got into their own cars, all the colours of boiled sweets, and they set off very slowly with the undertaker's assistant walking in front.

'He's never going to walk all the way?' asked Bea's uncle, astonished, knowing it was miles to the crematorium.

Bea giggled. 'He'll just go to the end of the road,' said Mother. 'Then he'll hop into the hearse and put his foot down.'

Her sister-in-law nudged her husband again to indicate 'There you are.' They couldn't care less, the pair of them. Laughing and joking . . . He flinched, irritably, wishing Billy were here with them in the car. Billy had never stood any nonsense from his sister and had always called him Fred. 'Call him Percy,' his sister had said. 'His name's Percy.' Billy had replied that he wouldn't call his worst enemy Percy, and he was going to call him Fred, and she could like it or lump it.

'Here we go again,' said Bea as they got out at the crematorium, to the tune of a song that went on – happy as can be. She shivered in the autumn cold. There was a smell of smoke on the air.

'Just look at the wreaths,' said her aunt, unctuously. 'Oh-h, aren't they lovely.' They were laid out on the floor along a sort of veranda around the chapel.

Bea looked at them, worried. She had always thought it was funny having flowers at funerals. They went with weddings and you could always give them away afterwards. People were pleased to be given wedding flowers, but these, which were really no different when you came to think of it, were bad luck. No one would take grave flowers. Then she began to wonder where these flowers were going anyway, for there would be no grave. Perhaps they'd stick them in the urn.

'What do they do with them, Mum?' she asked, trying to keep a straight face.

'I don't know,' said Mother. They stood outside discussing the possibilities – such as resale – Mother didn't like the idea of a second-hand wreath, but they'd smell awful if they were just thrown in a heap. 'Perhaps they bury them,' she said.

'In a *crematorium*?' said Bea.

'Well, perhaps they burn them,' said Mother, and they were off again.

All the mourners were already seated when they finally went in just before the six bearers – looking far glummer and more bereaved than the relations – entered with the coffin on their shoulders. The front row was taken up, and Mother and Bea had to sit in the second one.

Trust them, thought Bea's aunt, who was herself ensconced in the place of chief mourner. No organization and no respect.

Billy had run away to sea when he was sixteen and was in the battle of Zeebrugge a year later. He'd been skinny as anything then, but he'd weighed seventeen stone when he died. Mother wondered whether they had bigger, stronger bearers for big bodies, and whether the six men were swearing silently to themselves as they advanced down the aisle.

There was soft solemn music coming from somewhere, and the chapel felt curiously warm for the time of year. The minister emerged from behind a curtain, also wearing an extremely serious and sorrowful expression, as though all his own loved ones had died. He had to consult a piece of paper before he could remember the name of the dear departed brother in the place of honour on the trestles.

They sang 'For Those in Peril on the Sea', as it was the only nautical hymn Mother could think of, and Bea had to struggle to suppress a vision of herself leaping up and smashing a bottle of champagne on the prow of the coffin. She stared at her aunt's shoulders in the pew in front. They heaved occasionally. A long, narrow insect suddenly dropped from under the brim of her aunt's hat and hung sideways on her collar, pulsating slightly. If I tapped her on the shoulder, thought Bea, and told her there was something crawling down the back of her neck, she'd yell the place down; it'd brighten up the proceedings no end. The insect gleamed in the artificial light and idly flexed its legs. It seemed not to realize that it was intruding on a funeral. Bea was thinking about it when the coffin began to move. The music was still oozing in very slowly, like sweet thick medicine, but something had gone wrong with the machinery that took the dead to the nether regions. Instead of going at the usual ponderous pace, pregnant with awesome import, the coffin was whizzing along like some mad fairground thing. It shot through the terminal curtains with an irreligious crash and was gone. There was a frightful silence, broken only by a hysterical giggle – not Bea or Mother this time. They were staring in disbelief at the faintly moving curtains. I don't blame you, Dad, thought Bea, it was bloody boring. Not at all your style. I bet you hated every minute of it . . .

Trust you, Billy, Mother was thinking.

'I think it's *disgusting*,' said Bea's aunt almost before they were out. 'With what they charge now, you'd think they could do the thing properly. I'd ask for a refund, if I were you.'

Back at the house Mother took the tea cloths off the ham and the cream cakes and passed round plates and paper serviettes. Bea picked up the bottle of salad cream and shook it elaborately, and Mother laughed. 'I bet he's sorry he's not here,' she said, speaking of Bea's husband, away at sea. The first time Bea had brought him home they'd redecorated the lounge specially, and he'd picked up the tomato sauce and shaken it, and the top had come off and tomato sauce had exploded everywhere – on the table, the carpet, the new wallpaper. Billy had laughed so much he'd nearly fallen off his chair. He'd sat there rocking until he nearly cried, laughing.

Bea always said her husband had only married her for the sake of her dad. Her aunt was making a good tea, balancing a plate on her lap and cutting up her tomato and lettuce into little bits, while her eyes gleamed and glanced everywhere. She was wondering if she was to have anything – such as the old granite clock of their father's that she'd always begrudged to Billy and his family.

Bea leaned across and examined her aunt's collar. 'There was something crawling on you in the chapel,' she said.

'Eeeh,' said her aunt, shuddering and wriggling her shoulders.

'I thought I saw it drop on your ham,' said Bea. 'I can't see it now.' She peered down at the empty plate.

Billy hadn't left much. Mother wouldn't be well off. Bea remembered him after the first heart attack, lying on his back upstairs in bed. 'Come and sit here and I'll tell you a story,' he'd say. She'd sit on his bed for hours like a great big kid, forgetting the shopping and the housework. He used to lie there, flicking matchsticks right across the room on to the top of the wardrobe. 'If your ruddy mum ever complains I've left her nothing,' he'd say, 'tell her there's enough matches up there to light the fires for a year.'

Mother poured out the sherry. Dad had died on his way to the pub, and Bea had been so sorry that he hadn't had his pint and died on the way back.

After a while Mother started gathering up the dirty plates and taking them out to the scullery. She filled the sink with hot water and began to wash up with enormous care, scraping all the bits into the bin.

There was a knock at the open kitchen door, and there stood a little boy. 'Is Billy back yet?' he asked, being too young to understand.

Mother half-turned to shout 'Billy', before she remembered. Oh Billy, she thought, her hands dangling, suddenly still in the soapy water. Oh Billy, whatever are we going to do . . .

THE AUTHOR AND THE
AIR HOSTESS

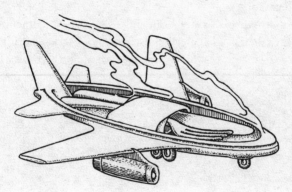

He had taken up writing in middle life, and as his style offered no problems of comprehension or interpretation to the average reader and his previous time had been spent in the world of finance, giving him a good sense of plot, he became very successful.

He wrote thrillers about brave, though ruthless, young men who, on the whole, were on the side of the right – in all senses of that word – and ruthless bad men who were on the wrong side. His women, good and bad, were beautiful, but the good women were unusually good and could always summon up a soft laugh even after the most extraordinary tribulations – torture, both mental and physical, and immersion in icy seas. Even after two days and nights tied by the hair to a hook in the wall of a rat-infested sewer, these women, emerging, would often utter a soft laugh.

On publication of his second bestseller, he divorced his old wife, who was very like his mother and had a loud, contemptuous laugh, and married a new one on the lines of his latest heroine, who was precisely similar to his earlier heroine except that her name was Sammy, not Debby. She was the daughter of his hero's boss, a faceless person of enormous importance to the military security of the West – a circumstance which naturally made Sammy extremely vulnerable and led to her often finding herself in situations of great discomfort and danger – at the mercy of a cold-eyed communist psychopath one moment and hanging by a thread from a helicopter over the Grampians the next. However, Sammy, apart from being perfectly lovely, was possessed of such radiant goodness that all who saw her, except for cold-eyed psychopaths who loved no one, loved her, and even crotchety hoteliers, on hearing her soft laugh, would serve her and her hero a meal in their bedroom in the small hours after one of these taxing experiences. Which was just as well, since the hero was frequently suffering from frostbite, rope burns, broken ribs, concussion – and, having been brutally kicked while helplessly strapped to an oil drum, was probably bleeding internally as well, though this was never mentioned; his urbanity remained unimpaired.

The new wife was called Sally and the Author met her on an aeroplane where she was a hostess. She was blonde, petite and enormously helpful, passing round sick bags with a kindly smile, leaning over seats to inquire about the well-being of old ladies going to see their married children and their kiddies; her freshly deodorized armpit offering no offence to the nearer passenger. She took more care of the passengers than you could possibly imagine, with a friendly word here, a reassuring touch there. She even had a soft laugh, as the Author noticed when a drunk accidentally spilled his drink over her skirt.

The Author had asked her to have dinner with him in South Africa when they arrived, and had explained that he was there to do research for his forthcoming novel. She had at once recognized his name since his books were widely available at airports, and had been impressed by his wealth and status and had determined, fractionally before he did, that they should be married.

Sally so closely resembled his construct, Sammy, that the Author began to imagine that he had invented her and that she had not existed until he had written down her vital statistics and imbued her with all the desirable feminine qualities, and he began to love her as many artists love their creations – with a breathless admiration, amounting almost to worship. Frequently he congratulated himself on his cleverness in forming such a perfectly rounded and truly female creature, until Sally, who actually was no fool – a bit rapacious, perhaps, with an eye to the main chance, but a normal, averagely intelligent girl – began to feel a little aggrieved.

Whoever it was who had made her (she was not religious) she was damn sure it wasn't the Author, and one day as he fingered her hair with a proprietorial gesture, remarking on its perfection of shade and depth of curl, she turned on him and snapped. He couldn't have been more surprised had one of his books leapt from the shelf and pinched his nose. He went into his study and closed the door; and it seemed likely he would stay there for ever, until towards evening he was inspired with the notion of making his current heroine, Kelly, into a girl not only lovely and good, but also a creature of dash and spirit. ('Oh Kelly, you're so beautiful when you're angry.')

Meanwhile Sally was regretting her harsh words, since she enjoyed her life with the Author – the clothes, the car, the house in Ireland; the MPs, the television people and occasional peer who came to dinner – and she was fond of him. But as she simmered down and stopped saying righteously to herself that she would rather be hated for what she was than loved for what she was not, she became aware that underneath her quite proper resentment was a superstitious fear, for she had read her husband's books and the heroines she so resembled were not only vapid beyond measure but were called upon to undergo most horrifyingly frightening trials, and Sally knew she would not survive a single one of these adventures in the sanguine fashion of Sammy, Debby and Kelly.

Then the cat disappeared. It had its breakfast as usual, went out and never came back. Sally found this awfully sinister. The Author had just completed an involved chapter in the current book concerning the kidnapping of his hero's cat. The minions of a foreign power – insensitive automata with no understanding of the Englishman's fondness for animals – had assumed that as it went with him everywhere it was probably the repository of microchips containing highly important top secret information. They took the cat to little bits, even looking inside its teeth – a self-defeating exercise since the hero was so enraged at their cruelty that when he caught up with them he was going to feel justified in behaving towards them more meanly than he would otherwise have done.

Sally hunted for the cat for days, beginning in the shrubbery, and then wandering far afield, asking everyone she met if they had seen it. She put an advert in the local paper's lost-and-found section, although she knew it was hopeless. These days only things lost were printed. No one would go to the trouble of reporting they had found something.

She began to wonder if her husband was a true master of the self-fulfilling prophecy. There were other coincidences. Small wars broke out in approximately those corners of the globe where he had set them in his book; high-ranking civil servants, closely resembling several of his minor characters, defected to the East.

Sally decided she must breach the web of fantasy. She would introduce her husband to her mother.

She had told him a little about her background – saying that her father had been in the army, which was true as he had been a sergeant in the Catering Corps – but had not thought it necessary to go into details. Her mother, she had said, lived in retirement at the seaside, without adding that what she had retired from was the profession of boarding-house landlady.

The Author had not been very interested, assuming, naturally, that his wife had sprung from the kind of milieu he would have written for her, but he didn't in the least mind going down to see her mother. Indeed, he said, since the poor lady hadn't been well enough to attend the wedding, it was time they paid her a visit. Sally hadn't told her about the wedding until it was over, but had since sent her a hamper of food from Harrods, explaining that because her intended was so famous the ceremony had had to be conducted in the utmost secrecy. She very much hoped that this had mollified her mother, an irascible person who was just as likely to take offence at a present of food as be grateful.

They drove to the coast on Saturday morning. The Author visualized a whitish villa fronting on the ocean, chintzy, faded by sea wind and perhaps a bottle of hock with lunch. He had gathered that Sally's mother was not well off. He wondered if she could even afford a woman to do the housework and asked idly whether she lived alone.

'Yes,' said Sally, shortly.

It must be very difficult for her, thought the Author, compassionately, living alone in that big house. He should have thought earlier of offering her some help, but then these old army families were proud.

Sally was regretting her impulse and toying with the idea of saying that she was suddenly very ill and must turn round and go home at once, but her superstitious fear of finding herself suspended over a jacuzzi full of piranha fish, or lashed to a cable in the path of an ascending ski lift, kept her silent. Also, she felt that in some way her self-respect was at stake, and so she sat in the passenger seat, biting the nail she kept for such emergencies, torn between nervousness and defiance.

The Author slowed down on the outskirts of town and asked for directions. 'Straight on,' said Sally. He was surprised, imagining that her home would have been further out on the cliffs. He was even more surprised as they drove through the decent residential district and came to boarding-house territory with signs offering B & B and meanly gaunt commercial hotels called Sea View and Ocean Prospect.

'Here,' said Sally. 'You can park round the corner.' She didn't speak again as they walked to what seemed to him the nastiest of all the nasty houses, its brickwork painted bright blue and its window-sills picked out in red. The front door was slightly ajar. 'Mum,' called Sally.

'Come on up,' responded a voice from halfway up the stairs.

'My mother has the second-floor flat,' explained Sally in a very correct voice. The stairs were laid with clean shiny lino, each tread protected by a metal strip.

'Well, my girl,' said the person waiting to welcome them in her doorway. 'So this is the feller. And about time too.' She laughed – a loud, almost contemptuous laugh.

'Hello, Mum,' said Sally in a suddenly different voice, and she kissed her.

'I haven't got anything in,' said her mother. 'You've got younger legs than me. Nip down to Mrs Macs and get three cod and chips. D'you like mushy peas?' she asked the Author. He said he didn't, although he didn't know, never having tried them.

'Hang on,' said Sally's Mum to her daughter, reaching for her handbag from the sideboard.

'Let me . . .' said the Author, finding his voice and feeling for his wallet.

'Get away with you,' said Sally's Mum in rough affectionate tones. 'This is on me.' She sat him down in a cut-moquette and varnished-wood chair and gave him a glass of British sherry.

They left after a tea of fish-paste sandwiches and chocolate cake, left over from the Harrods parcel. The Author, in a way, had quite enjoyed himself, since Sally's Mum was a loquacious and amusing woman. The real trouble was that she reminded him of someone and halfway through the afternoon he had realized that that someone, despite the vast cultural difference, was his previous wife. Once he had started thinking about resemblances, he had realized that his new wife very much resembled her mother. So as he got into the car he gave a soft – rather hollow – laugh.

THE STATUE

There has been a lot of talk recently about statues moving. Well they *do*. I know because I once spent Christmas in a niche. I had been shopping yet again on the endless Christmas round and I stopped at our local church for a sitdown more than anything else because I was in no mood for praying. I sat there going over my purchases in my mind and realizing I would have to go out yet again since I had forgotten many things – wrapping paper, and cloves for the bread sauce and red apples for the centre of the table and more mundane things like cats' meat and toothpaste. As I collected my carrier bags and genuflected preparatory to leaving I glanced to my left and caught the gaze of our local saint; her mellifluous, impartial and, as I now thought, annoyingly smug gaze.

'It's all right for you,' I told her. 'Stuck up there out of the way in your plastered peace with your self-satisfied smirk.' I would never have spoken like that normally but my feet were hurting and my arms were nearly dragged out of their sockets with the weight of the shopping. It was freezing outside too. Still, that was no excuse for being rude to a saint so I apologized in an undertone, and then just as I turned to go I saw her eyes look swiftly to the left and right and then she put her painted plaster finger to her painted plaster mouth and leaned forward towards me. Naturally I was astounded. I dropped one of my bags and heard something break and I gripped the back of a pew for support. Luckily there were very few other people in the church, only one or two old women rapt in contemplation of Our Lady and a comatose wino laid out on the floor. All the same, at my reaction she straightened up and resumed her stance in her niche, gazing into the distance with her small smile. After a moment I addressed her again. 'Did you just move,' I demanded, in a whisper, 'or am I going mad on top of everything else?' Her eyes flickered down at me and her smile widened. I sat on the pew and looked sideways and up at her, and then I heard her speak. The gist of what she said was this: that she would carry my shopping home and take my place over Christmas if I would agree to take her place in the niche. Well, it wasn't exactly up to my dream of spending Christmas alone in a small snowbound hotel at the end of the world, but it would certainly mean a rest, so I hardly hesitated at all before agreeing and the next thing I knew I was looking across the church from the saint's erstwhile vantage point with my eyes on a level with the seventh Station of the Cross and a weary-looking woman was gathering up a lot of carrier bags and genuflecting below my feet. As she left she smiled up at me reassuringly and told me not to worry, she would take very good care of everyone and everything of mine. I had a moment's misgiving because my motives in agreeing to this imposture had been completely selfish, arising from my great tiredness, from the prospect of for once being spared Uncle Fred's Christmas jokes, Cousin Amy's dissatisfaction with the arrangements no matter what they might be, and the early morning riot as the children tore the wrappings from their presents and discovered that I had forgotten to buy batteries to motivate their robots, toy cars, radios, etc. But then I reflected that my family could hardly be in better hands than those of a canonized saint and that if I had any sense I would stop worrying and make the most of my rest. It would be ungrateful to spend Christmas fretting about those things I had left undone. I hoped the saint would be inspired to check the store cupboards and discover the lack of cloves. Bread sauce without cloves is insipid. Then I began to relax. The cat would point out unhesitatingly the lack of cats' meat; if anyone could not get by without toothpaste then they could hasten out and buy some. I felt the saint could be trusted to choose some decorative motif for the table centre, and as for the wrapping paper – well, I found I really didn't care about that any more. I was perfectly comfortable standing in the niche because, after all, I had no bone or muscle to strain or stretch, being composed of plaster and paint on a wire armature, and I felt warm and secure in the silence which was stirred only by an occasional shuffle of ancient feet, a cough, a murmured incantation. I clutched my handful of plaster hyacinths (the saint's most potent emblem) and gazed with her own tranquillity across the aisles, my foot resting gently on a plaster boar's head.

Suddenly I became aware that someone was addressing me. I cautiously lowered my gaze and saw the top of a woman's head, nodding slowly up and down. '. . . I wouldn't want him to suffer,' she was saying, 'not too much anyway, for when he hasn't the drink taken he's been good enough to me.' At this she looked up, her eyes met mine and I recognized her as my next-door neighbour's cleaning lady. Simultaneously I realized that she was invoking the help of her whom she believed to be the saint, to procure the death of her husband; had probably been doing a novena to this end, and I felt very much taken aback although not entirely surprised. The saint, you see, had gained her eminence in the community of saints not merely by the exemplary virtue of her ways but because she had been married by force to a perfect brute who used to beat her and tie her to trees and fling her down into dungeons because she utterly refused to fulfil her conjugal obligations. One day while he was chasing her round the woods she ran into a wild boar who gored her to death; only just before she expired in a handy bed of hyacinths she forgave her husband his importunities, cruelties and misdemeanours, and he repented and mended his ways amazingly, becoming a highly respected member of society and exceedingly devout. I was aware that some uneducated women, misunderstanding this tale and forgetting the saint's magnanimity and remembering only the horrible ways of her husband, were in the habit of asking her for assistance in marital matters, but I had not realized that anyone could be so misguided as to seek her intercession to the extent of asking for the death of a spouse. My shock must have shown on my face for I felt my jaw drop and at that moment the woman looked imploringly up at me. My fingers momentarily relaxed and I felt a hyacinth slip from between them. Of course, the woman shrieked. I knew just how she felt. If I hadn't been so tired I might have shrieked myself when the saint spoke to me. The woman fled up the side aisle to the door and a moment later she was back, dragging the curate with her. He had clearly been interrupted in the course of his tea for he was eating bread and jam, and had the reluctant air of a curate who knows that the cake will have been eaten by the time he returns.

'Look,' said the woman dramatically, pointing at the wretched hyacinth.

'It's only a hyacinth,' said the curate. The clergy are notoriously sceptical about miraculous happenings. They have to be.

'*She* dropped it on me,' insisted the woman, pointing up at me while I strove very hard to keep in countenance, much regretting my lapse although I felt I could not be held wholly to blame since she had greatly startled me. One does not expect one's neighbour's char to nurture murderous inclinations towards her husband, or at least not to be so open and frank about them. I had to remind myself that she supposed me to be the saint and not her employer's neighbour but I still considered the behaviour indiscreet.

She and the curate argued this way and that and the tone of their discussion became quite heated. I stood in some embarrassment, vowing to be more careful until Christmas had passed. When I was alone again, reflecting on the nature of marriage, I had another worrying thought. My husband was an uxorious man and in view of the saint's attitude to conjugality I could see the possibility of serious misunderstanding. I hoped she would have the foresight to develop a heavy cold and insist on sleeping in the spare room.

The next morning as the congregation arrived for Mass I kept a wary eye on the door to see the saint enter in the guise of myself. She had brought the two older children and I was relieved to see that her – my – nose was scarlet and our eyes were streaming. After Mass she came over to speak to me. In between a muttered Ave and a Paternoster and over the clicking of the beads she whispered reassurances to me about the state of the house and the children's appetites and my husband's health. Even the cat, it seemed, had accepted her without question. I longed to ask her if she had remembered to buy the cloves but after the events of the afternoon I dared not and stood smiling vacantly as she spoke to me in my own voice.

'Come *on*, Mummy,' said my children, pulling at my skirt which the saint wore and I felt a tremor in my plaster toes until I reminded myself that Mummy was, for the moment, not I but the tired-looking woman below with the dreadful cold.

'Goodbye, hyacinth lady,' said the younger of the two older children and I was glad to see that I – she – punished this affectation with a little shake. Relieved of anxiety about my family I reverted to worrying about my neighbour's char. She was a nice, hard-working woman with many children and, as had now become evident, a husband so unbearable that she wished him dead. I would not have been so concerned had she not confided in me, for although she did not know that I had her secret I felt strangely responsible for her. She came to look at me again on her way home from work, standing at my feet and gazing up at me with an expression of half-fearful expectancy. I was dreadfully tempted to speak to her, to offer her – not comfort, for I could think of none – but advice. I wanted to tell her to go to a marriage guidance counsellor although I knew that the fact that she had come to me – or rather the saint – meant that if this idea had occurred to her she had rejected it. She looked at me imploringly for a little while longer and then left, her poor shoulders bowed with worry and disappointment and the prospect of a beating from her husband and I seethed in my niche with indignation and pity.

The next day was Christmas Eve and the saint called to see me in the afternoon with two of the younger children. She sat in the pew below me while the children went to look at the crib – at the lambs and the donkey and the star. She whispered that everything was ready for tomorrow, the capon stuffed, the potatoes peeled, the oyster soup ready to be reheated. Yes, she said kindly, she knew she must be sure and let it boil, she promised she wouldn't let my family suffer from food poisoning – not even Uncle Fred or Cousin Amy. I was glad to see she had a sense of humour and relieved that she seemed to have a good grasp of the basic rules of cookery. This worry had not occurred to me before but as she had flourished some centuries ago I would not have been surprised had she confessed an inability to master the intricacies of the gas stove, the food processor, washing-machine, etc. I wondered if she'd been driving the car. The evening passed peacefully and I stood, half-dreaming, content in my niche while one or two people asked my intercession in more reasonable matters – a girl wished to visit the Costa Brava and an old man wanted to win some money on a horse. I made a note to pass these requests on to the saint when we resumed our normal roles and personae. As the time for Midnight Mass approached I watched the saint come in with all my family, even Uncle Fred and Cousin Amy, right down to the baby who peered at me over his father's shoulder with every sign of approval. Taking a chance, I blew him a swift kiss and he remarked 'poggelich bah' and laughed.

'Sh,' said my husband.

'Pooh,' said my child, beaming at me. I pulled myself together and stood quite still, gazing over their heads at the far wall.

Halfway through Mass there was a slight disturbance at the back of the church as some latecomers arrived. From the stumbling and slurred mutterings I gathered that they were drunk. This happened every year. Certain men who never attended Mass at any other time, not even to make their Easter Duties, would invariably, inevitably, roll up, paralytic, for Midnight Mass. Nobody minded as long as they weren't sick and didn't swear too loudly as they fell over attempting to kneel unsupported on the floor. One of them reeled unsteadily down the aisle and came to a halt below my niche. He clutched the end of the pew and knelt down. As he did so I caught sight of his face and recognized him despite the crossed eyes and hectically flushed nose as the husband of my neighbour's char. I glared down at him before recalling myself to the Mass. When it was over and the sleepy congregation made its slow way to the doors I saw that he had fallen fast asleep leaning against the pew's end. No one made any move to disturb him, but left unanimously by way of the centre aisle as he slumped there, snoring gently, and suddenly I was seized by an irresistible compulsion. Cautiously I loosened yet another hyacinth and dropped it on his head. He woke disoriented, half-blind with beer and sleep, and looked round pugnaciously. Whereupon I leaned swiftly forward, seized him by the collar so that he was forced to look into my face, and remarked in a low but positive tone, 'If you don't stop drinking and beating your wife, you bastard, you will be very, very sorry.' Then I dropped him and stood back in the niche, stone-still and silent. I heard later that he had left the church, gone home and kissed his wife and all his children, thrown away the cans of beer he was keeping in the sideboard, helped wash up after Christmas dinner and taken his whole family for an outing on Boxing Day. His wife never knew exactly what had happened but she was delighted. When he stopped drinking he was able to go back to being a builder's labourer and he made so much money that she was able to give up her job cleaning for my neighbour and stay at home washing his labouring clothes. My neighbour was very put out but I felt that that really couldn't be helped.

The saint came back the day after Boxing Day. I thought that she – I – looked very tired but she seemed content and said that she had left everything as she imagined I would wish to find it and Cousin Amy had not been too obnoxious. There were quite a few leftovers still, but she was sure I would be able to sort everything out when I got home. She apologized that the bread sauce had been a bit tasteless because she hadn't been able to find my cloves but everything else had been very good. When she was back in her niche and I in my self I thought that she looked rather relieved, and I was a bit annoyed to find that she had left me with the remains of her cold, although she had got over the initial worst stages of sore throat, raw chest and itching nose.

I found the house remarkably tidy, with an unusual air of order and propriety; the children cheerful and amiable. Only the baby was sitting in his pram, thumb in mouth, looking puzzled and faintly forlorn. When I picked him up he looked at me for a long moment, then took his thumb out of his mouth, put his arms around my neck and would not be parted from me until he fell asleep long past his bedtime when the moon was high.

AN ARABIAN NIGHT

Somebody said, 'Tell me a story.'
  So I did. This is it.

She said, 'Tell me a story.'
  'Do what?' he said.
  She said, 'I'm bored.'
  'So watch telly,' he said.
  She said, 'It's all in Arabic.'
  'So read the paper,' he said.
  She said, 'I've read it three times already. I'm bored.'
He was leaning over the balcony watching the others on the terrace below. He was bored, too. Sooner or later on holiday everybody is bored, but the responsible adult does not admit it. Certainly not when he's paid an arm and a leg for the privilege. 'Then let's go down and join the others,' he said.
  She said, 'We came up here to get away from the others.' She was beginning to whine. Two days in a small town under the Mountains of the Moon and already she was whining. He liked it no better than she did but he wasn't saying. He was paying. Yet it was not her ingratitude that irked him but her stupidity. Did she not know that the first rule of holiday-making is to insist that you are enjoying yourself (especially if the holiday is costing your companion a certain amount of money), no matter what the circumstances. Ice-bound in a glacier, tormented by a wild simoom – if the purpose of your

presence is holiday-making then somehow or other, by hook or by crook, you must give the impression that you are enjoying it. Otherwise you look a fool. Wherever the constraints of work impel you, you may complain – hotels with towels so thick and so soft you could curl up and sleep in them, morning tea in a four-poster – if you are amongst these delights in the course of earning money you are permitted, nay expected, to find fault. Whereas on holiday even the slug in your tomato must be regarded as a matter for amusement – for approval and mirth – and be stored away as the stuff of anecdote. Well, that was his view, anyway. When he bothered to think about it.

'I'm going down,' he said. 'Have a drink, stretch my legs, see what's going on.'

She said, 'There's nothing going on,' and then thought that perhaps she had gone too far, so followed him downstairs to the bar and the terrace beyond.

'Oh there you are,' said a number of voices. 'Wondered where you'd got to.' 'What did you make of the casbah?' etc.

'Not a lot,' he said, appearing to break his rule. Actually he was adhering to another rule, which was not to get too matey with the others on the tour.

'Oh, come on,' they said, 'what about the water-sellers, and the snake-charmer, and the little boy selling aphrodisiacs in the souk?'

'Yes,' he said, but he was thinking about the high mud walls of the houses and wondering what lay beyond.

They sat a little apart from the others and she reached out and touched his arm. 'Go on then,' she said, 'tell me a story.'

'I know a good one,' called somebody.

'She thinks you're Nebuchadnezzar,' said someone else.

'Scheherazade,' corrected a woman.

On tours like this, he reflected, the women were always

better-educated than the men. They probably had more time. He went to the bar and bought two long, cold lagers. Boredom was beginning to make him irritable.

'Say one of us was a murderer . . .' he began and a girl cried 'ooh' – not his; she was looking at him silently – '. . . and he was on the run.'

'Or her,' said his girl.

'Who's telling this story?' he asked.

She shut up again.

'Say I was a murderer,' he said, 'and I have to get away from the consequences. Could I lose myself among the people?'

'Not if you didn't speak the language,' said a practical man drinking orange juice.

'I do speak the language,' he said, 'as well as Lawrence spoke it.'

'I've just been reading him,' said someone who appeared of indeterminate sex in the North African night. 'Couldn't see what all the fuss was about.'

'T.E. Lawrence,' he explained. 'I speak the language and mingle with the people and I'm taken for a native except for my blue eyes.'

'You haven't got blue eyes,' objected his girl.

'You couldn't eat the food,' said someone.

'Passport,' said someone else.

'Money,' said yet a third.

'I make my money as a storyteller,' he explained. 'I sit in the souk and tell stories and they give me food and money. Who needs a passport?'

'You couldn't eat the . . .' interrupted a fat man and was told to 'Sh.'

'You can't tell stories,' said his girl. 'I asked you to tell me a story and you told me to watch telly.'

They cried 'Sh' to her as well. Somebody brought him a whisky and several of them said, 'Go on.' It wasn't so much that he had got their attention as that each of them wished to pick holes in his story, improve on it and offer their own version.

'I am a particularly brilliant storyteller,' he said loudly. He looked round at them in the light that came from the bar and they all closed their mouths, waiting. 'And a positively marvellous murderer,' he added.

'You're so conceited,' said his girl. 'Who did you murder?'

He thought for a moment. 'You, probably,' he said. 'You drove me to it with your insatiable demands for a story, so I pushed you in the pool or maybe I strangled you in a corner of the Djmaa el F'naa and left you for the dogs to find.'

'A lot of husbands murder their wives,' said someone out of the purest politeness. It was always as well to honour the proprieties on these tours. You never knew quite what the relationships were.

'Why can't *I* murder *you*?' asked his girl. 'For being so boring.'

'I'm stronger than you,' he said.

'But I'm more cunning,' said his girl.

'I don't know why you think that,' he said. 'I find you rather obvious.'

'What happens if the dogs don't find her?' asked the reader of D.H. Lawrence. 'What if the police find her?'

'I haven't seen a lot of police,' said a woman. 'I think they use the army.'

'They've got police,' said someone else. 'I saw two this morning with rifles standing in the souk by the copper beaters.'

Somebody laughed aloud and felt it necessary to apologize. '*Copper* beaters,' she explained. 'You know – coppers. Sorry.' There was a short, rebuke-laden silence.

'I'm not as obvious as you,' said his girl, who had clearly been brooding over this for some minutes in the hope of being inspired with a witty reply. 'You're *terribly* obvious.'

This was not merely not witty but rather heavier than, on the face of it, the situation required.

'The dogs *do* find her,' he said. 'This is *my* story. They eat her all up except for the palms of her hands.'

'That's not your story,' complained the cultivated woman who knew the difference between Nebuchadnezzar and Scheherazade. 'That's Jezebel.'

'I was walking under the house walls,' he said, 'minding my own business and watching the chickens scratching when she came running up behind me and asked me to tell her a story . . .'

'You can't tell stories,' his girl said, on the verge of tears. 'You can't do anything.'

Somebody called to a passing waiter and ordered her a whisky. Someone else reached over and patted her hand. The party was getting friendlier than it should.

'So what I did,' he said, 'was throw dust in her eyes, and then do you know what I did?'

'What?' they cried. 'What did you do?'

'Why,' he said, 'I ran away. I ran up the steps in the mud wall, past the chickens, through a big wooden door studded with iron nails, until I came out into a garden. I'm not really a murderer – not yet.'

'How long were you up there?' asked the clever one.

'Hours,' he said dreamily. 'Hours and hours.'

'Well, that's not true,' remarked several people. 'You were with us the whole time. You couldn't have been more than a few minutes.'

'He's telling lies,' said his girl in a stronger tone. 'He does tell lies.'

'Stories,' he protested, 'I'm a storyteller. Remember?'

'Then what happened?' they asked.

'It was a garden,' he said, 'with flowers all round the walls and growing in big jars. There was a fountain in the middle and the cool splash of silken drops . . .'

'Ha,' said his girl scornfully.

'Sh,' they said. 'Go on.'

'. . . and under a silken canopy . . .'

'Awful lot of silk,' said his girl.

'Under a silken canopy were long divans covered in sumptuous materials, all the colours of the Orient.'

'Silk, I suppose,' said his girl, and somebody else quietly filled her glass from his own.

'Tasselled, embroidered cushions stuffed with the down of ducks . . .' That didn't sound quite right. He amended it. 'Stuffed with the down of peacocks – and before anyone says peacocks don't have down, let me explain that they do. It grows round their bottoms, beneath their tail feathers, and you need two thousand peacocks to fill a single cushion. There are many girls who do nothing all their lives but pluck the down from the bums of peacocks.'

'Doesn't it hurt?' asked the reader of D.H. Lawrence.

'They give them arak to stun them first,' he said. 'It soon grows again and they don't feel a thing.'

'It sounds cruel but beautiful,' said D.H. Lawrence.

'It was all intensely beautiful. The scents, the colours, the sound of the fountain, the food . . .'

'What did you eat?' asked the fat man, suspiciously.

'Couscous,' he said, 'and pigeons, grilled over fragrant herbs. Peppers and okra and aubergine and a whole baby lamb stewed with almonds and wrapped in vine leaves.'

'I wouldn't touch any of that,' said the fat man. 'I know people laugh at me but I like to stick to what they call international cuisine. I know it's unadventurous, and you may ask why I travel at all if I don't want to try everything, but I tell you I *like* travel – I like new places and the sun, only my stomach won't take all that foreign stuff. I've tried it, and the time I've spent regretting it you wouldn't believe – that's why I always stay in this sort of hotel. You know what you're getting.'

D.H. Lawrence turned on him savagely. 'If all you want is fish and chips and gammon and pineapple and prawn cocktail, why don't you stay at home?' she hissed. Her very vehemence now made it obvious that she was female.

The fat man was hurt and astonished. 'I've just been explaining . . .' he said, and the girl who had asked for a story took advantage of this interruption to state that she'd seldom heard anything so boring as all this drivel about peacocks and peppers. The waiter was hailed yet again and her glass replenished.

The storyteller took up his tale. 'There were tiles on the pavements and the low walls – blue and green and yellow and white – shining in the sun where the jasmine and the oleanders parted their boughs, and in the shade lay a great silken – a great lithe-limbed – cat such as I never saw before.'

'Oh, nuts,' said his girl.

'On the low tables lay vast bowls of cerulean blue, containing fruit – mangoes and paw-paws, and apples and breadfruit, and . . .'

'How about some kiwi fruit?' said his girl.

'I wouldn't touch the fruit myself,' said the fat man. 'My parents were out in India. They washed everything in permanganate of potash. Otherwise – cholera.'

D.H. Lawrence snorted.

'Did you meet anyone?' asked the cultivated lady, thinking of Burton.

The storyteller hesitated. He put up a hand to hide a smile. 'There was a dragoman,' he said. 'There was a sort of butler in a djellaba and soft slippers with curled-up toes, who went round seeing to the hookahs. There were flocks of white doves too, and parakeets in cages.' He wondered whether to introduce an aviary of nightingales and decided against it. 'There were roses and jasmine . . .'

'You said that,' said his girl.

'. . . there was a spreading date palm with its roots in the earth, growing right up through the whole house until it met the sky.'

'But did you *talk* to anyone?' asked the lady of culture.

He hesitated again, not wishing to come too soon to the whole point of his story. 'Somebody brought me a silver dish with almonds, and *loukoum* and candied violets . . .'

'What hookers?' asked his girl suddenly.

'He means hubble-bubbles,' said the lady of culture. 'You saw them this morning outside the cafés.'

'If you ate all that sweet muck,' said the fat man, 'you won't fancy your dinner. Tonight it's Waldorf salad, boeuf bourgignon, and Black Forest gâteau.'

'*I* don't fancy Moroccan Black Forest gâteau,' said somebody in the shadows.

'They import it,' said the fat man. 'Fly it in from Germany.'

'*What* hookers?' asked the girl, who had now drunk so much that she could no longer listen. All she could do was catch a significant word here and there, latch on to it and worry it to death.

'Not hookers – *hookahs*,' they told her.

'You wouldn't think he was practically old enough to be my grandfather, would you?' she asked. 'Not the way he carries on, not the things he says. You'd think he was just a boy in the prime of his life, to listen to the way he talks, wouldn't you?'

'I don't think boyhood is the same as prime of life,' remarked an unexpected pedant.

The storyteller saw his chance slipping away. Unless he regained the centre of the stage the others would strike up the usual general conversation, and his girl would fall drunkenly asleep with her head on the table.

'She was tall,' he said. 'Her face was as the face of the moon . . .'

'Who was?' asked someone.

'. . . the lady who brought in the Turkish delight,' he said. 'Her eyes were as the eyes of night and her figure was as the figure of a young gazelle. She was clad in golden and azure silks . . .' He paused, but his girl was fishing for a glacé cherry in somebody else's glass. '. . . on her feet were silver sandals and around her neck hung a rope of rubies, big as hen's eggs. She knelt beside me and addressed me thus: "Oh, my love and my dream and my liver . . ."'

'Her *liver*?' asked the fat man.

'It's what these girls call their lovers,' explained the story-teller. 'They don't call them "My heart", they call them "My liver".'

'That's right,' said the lady of culture. 'It's in Burton. Everyone knows that.'

'It sounds disgusting,' said D.H. Lawrence.

'No worse than *heart*,' said the storyteller. 'It's all offal, anyway. The Greeks thought the spleen was the seat of emotions.'

The lady of culture wasn't certain about this so remained silent.

'She removed my shoes and washed my feet . . .'

'You're such a liar,' said his girl drowsily. 'I want my dinner.' She got up and they all felt they had to follow, so they dined early.

She sobered up over dinner and as they walked back to their room she said, 'Why did you have to tell that stupid story?'

'You asked me to,' he said.

'I didn't mean that one,' she said. 'I wanted you to go on with the one about murdering me. I didn't come into that other story at all. It was all pigeons and hookers and roses and livers. You don't care about me at all. You don't even love me enough to murder me. Anyone else would've murdered me and then put out their own eyes in remorse and gone to live in the desert. You just don't care . . .'

If she'd been permitted to go on, he felt, she might have proved almost as good a storyteller as he was himself, so, as they were presently passing the hotel swimming-pool, he pushed her in.

No, I don't know what happened next. I don't know whether she sank or swam. I don't care. I've told my story and you can make what you will of it. You can fish her out, if you like, and dry her in a big soft towel, and put her to bed in a four-poster, but I wouldn't if I were you.

She was really a very tiresome girl with her 'Tell me a story.'

JUDGE NOTT AND THE DWARF

He was called Dr Watts Ayling. It wasn't his name but it was what she called him. He hadn't got a spade beard and bifocals either, but as far as she was concerned he had. She often thought that she hated him quite badly, and wondered why she went on seeing him twice a week at enormous cost to her husband and inconvenience to herself – always going by bus instead of taxi out of some obscure self-punitive motive – and enduring the painful embarrassment of the analyst's queries. She had no intention whatsoever of permitting him the smallest insight into her unconscious, which was guarded by an extremely hostile and dangerous dwarf who raced round the ramparts of her psyche, armed to the teeth, eyes flashing, constantly alert and poised to parry any question which might offer a threat to the integrity of her neurosis, which was meanwhile languishing peacefully in an oubliette far, far down in unbroken darkness.

Her husband had suggested that possibly the whole business was a waste of time since it had been going on for months now and she was no different. She had responded with great anger because, she suspected, she hated her husband even more than her psychiatrist and lived only to annoy him. He was a member of the judiciary and in her mind she always called him Judge Nott, although, of course, that wasn't his name. He organized her life for her completely and ruled her with a rod of disapproval, as hard and unyielding as iron.

Dr Watts Ayling looked tired. He said to her, 'Did you telephone me about ten minutes before you got here?'

She told him gently that ten minutes before she had arrived she had been on the bus and you couldn't really telephone people from buses – there weren't the facilities.

He smiled wearily as though he didn't believe her and she wondered briefly who it was who telephoned him and then hung up before he could answer. He had asked her several times if she'd been telephoning and she had explained that, on the whole, if she wished to communicate with a person by telephone she waited for a suitable time before despairing of a response, that if she were truly determined to speak to this person she persevered until she found them at home, and that she then did not hang up without saying anything. Nor, she had added silently to herself, do I ring your doorbell and run away. But she hadn't spoken aloud because a gesture from the dwarf had warned her that it could be dangerous and might present Dr Watts Ayling with the end of a thread which then just might lead him to that *hortus conclusus* which the dwarf guarded so fiercely.

The good doctor was now asking her about her father and she relaxed. This was perfectly safe. She said again that her father had been very nice and very kind and now was very dead, and that no, she didn't think that people who were nice and kind automatically got to be dead. She thought that everyone got to be dead; even total bastards. Even Judge Nott would die, she said with satisfaction, since this too was perfectly safe to impart. The person who called her in constantly from the garden and up from the cellar, insisting she should keep her little socks white, and demanding, like Dr Watts Ayling, that she should be all present and correct, would die and be thrown to the dark. He'd hate that, she said. He liked light, and order, and people working hard and together in serried ranks. He liked everyone to know that life was real and life was earnest, and if it wasn't raining now it soon would be. She was herself very idle, she explained, and she liked above all things to be left alone. Here she became aware of some agitation in the dwarf and caught herself up, falling silent. The dwarf was right. She could sense, although she couldn't see him since he was sitting behind her head, that the doctor had assumed the overall demeanour of a person patting himself on the back. He had done this once or twice before when her guard had been down for a moment. It annoyed her very much but it drove the dwarf to the point of frenzy, being far worse than the doctor's customary expression of sage benevolence.

Conciliatorily she began to explain to Dr Watts Ayling that her husband's militaristic bossiness and excessive judiciousness hardly worried her at all. 'He is,' she said airily, 'what we psychiatrists describe as an anal sadist and as such we do not need to concern ourselves with him any further.'

Dr Watts Ayling put in his little piece about how much he liked the glimpses of the Real Her that he was occasionally permitted to glimpse and announced that time was up. Hypocritical oaf, she said to herself, grinning secretly; and the dwarf gibbered and grimaced from the well-trodden battlements.

As she left, the telephone began to ring. 'That'll be me,' she said, 'telephoning from the bus.'

Just before she was due to leave home for her next session her own telephone rang. Her husband answered it and came to her – looking, for him, rather shaken and concerned. He stared her right in the eye and said that had been her psychiatrist's receptionist and there wouldn't be any session today because he was dead – murdered.

'*Murdered*,' she marvelled. 'How extraordinary.' She wondered if his bifocals were broken and whether there was blood drying on his spade beard. The paper next day said everyone

was baffled – his wife and receptionist at the motivelessness of
the attack, and the police at the peculiar nature of the injuries,
which they said, bewilderedly, seemed to have been inflicted
by a child or someone remarkably small of stature.

She wondered if she should tell them about the telephone
calls but decided against it, not wishing to get involved. It was
probable, she thought, that when they caught the malefactor it
would be before Judge Nott that he would be arraigned.

AN OLD-FASHIONED GIRL

Lou was an enchanting girl, as fair and gentle as a saint or an angel, or a virgin, blue-smocked against a golden sky with trusting hares and little doting birds, and flowers growing close to her hem. Her parents adored her, and even her sisters found her not too intolerable, which is unusual among sisters. They agreed between themselves that she was deficient in some way, that she lacked several human characteristics. She had never shown evidence of envy or anger and never argued. If she hadn't been one of themselves they might have described her as half-witted. As it was, they accepted her, protected her and teased her only occasionally. Sometimes they observed, rather resentfully, that in many ways she behaved as though she were an only child. Surely they were sufficiently bright and brilliant to deserve just a little jealousy, remarkable enough to make their pretty sister feel just a little inferior and afraid?

But Lou seemed unaware that she was letting her sisters down and passed through her childhood and her girlhood with none of the usual catastrophes and upheavals. In only one way did she refuse to conform: she wouldn't eat meat and her mother worried about her, fearing that she was becoming anorexic. Her sisters inwardly rejoiced at this symptom of rebellion until she explained in her simple fashion that she had no strong feelings about other people eating flesh if it did not trouble their consciences, but that she could not bring herself to dine on anything that had once had a face, that might have

113

met her eyes with its own. It would make her very sick, she said, and the big blue eyes to which she had referred filled with tears of anguished pity at the thought of all those dying faces.

When she was nineteen she got married. Her sisters were not as annoyed at this as they might have been before the rise of feminism. Typical of Lou, they said, to tie herself down at such an early age. They themselves were determined to enjoy life to the full and take every possible advantage of what it had to offer before selling themselves into bondage. Silly little Lou, they said, to go and get *married* of all things.

It was a delightful wedding, even before it had properly begun, as they waited in the churchyard. The sky was as blue as Lou's eyes and the sun shone on her with a kind of gentle fervour. In her white dress she seemed all golden. The corn in the distant fields was golden and so, when the time came to drink it, was the wine. The trees, rough and dark-skinned as they were, stood at a decent distance and pretended for the moment that their only purpose was to house numberless singing birds who fluttered and trilled in praise of marriage.

On the whole both families were pleased with the match. Lou's mother, as her second-born promised to love, honour and *obey*, smiled wistfully at the old-fashioned phrase. So did most of the congregation except for the bridesmaids who were, of course, Lou's sisters: they snarled and scowled but nobody noticed because they were all looking at Lou. When the ring was slipped on Lou's finger her mother, feeling that a chapter had been closed, sighed in relief and gave no thought to what the rest of the book might hold. She had that quality commonly ascribed to the animal kingdom, of believing that when things went well it would always be so. She felt the same when they went badly, which had led her to suspect that she might be melancholic in temperament, since by its very nature this quality disabled her from remembering the good times. Now, however, she had forgotten the bad times and the existence of evil in the universe. All was set fair and she was enjoying wearing her new hat, which was most becoming.

The mother of the groom was less sanguine, as mothers of the groom tend to be, but even she thought her son had chosen well and was fairly satisfied.

The groom was dark and, like most of his generation, very spoilt.

Lou had decided on pale sweet-pea colours for her brides-maids' frocks, and her elder sister, who was blonde like Lou, looked so pretty that the best man nearly proposed to her until she laughed at him. In his hired suit, she said, he looked like a pox doctor's clerk. The groom's mother, overhearing, thought it unlikely that the sisters of her new daughter-in-law would ever marry. Milly, the younger, was not blonde but tall, dark and handsome and she looked incongruous in her sweet-pea frock: she knew this and was bad-tempered in consequence. As the afternoon wore on she grew vehement in her opinion that marriage was an outmoded institution and went round telling people so. Her mother, seeing her in so foul a temper on this loveliest of all days, took her aside and asked – in a voice trembling between reproach and anxiety – whether she was jealous of Lou.

Milly's scorn at this suggestion, the contemptuous sneer that twisted up her face, were so vehement that her mother simply could not decide whether it was sour grapes or whether Milly truly did not care for grapes, be they sour or sweet. With one of her sudden changes of mood she began to worry that her youngest daughter might not be *normal*.

As the happy couple left on their honeymoon everyone threw things. Milly, overarm, threw an old shoe and hit the bridegroom, who half-turned from the car door and threw it back.

'Don't talk to strangers,' called the family, as they bent to pick up the litter.

Lou applied herself to marriage like an angel or a saint, with total commitment. Those of her friends whom her husband did not like, she dropped; and she was always there when he wanted her, never going anywhere before first telling him and always back when she should be. She would run his bath for him and wash his hair. Had he worn slippers she would have warmed them. Had he worn a hat and carried an umbrella she would have been waiting with them at the door when he left for the office – had he worked in an office. The truth was, Lou was an old-fashioned girl and believed that a wife should take over where her mother-in-law had been compelled to leave off. It worried her to think that her husband should suffer any diminution of comfort simply because he had exchanged a mother for a wife.

She inquired among his family and friends to discover his favourite dishes and made cottage pie every week, until he said, smiling, that he was beginning to feel like a cottage, and could they possibly have a change?

She cooked him steak and fillets of pork, and stuck bits of garlic and rosemary into legs of lamb for dinner parties, and prepared bacon and egg for his breakfast on Sundays.

The sight and smell of meat made her sick and it took all her fortitude to enter butchers' shops and then, at home in her own kitchen, handle the pathetic, horrible remnants of warm animals. As time passed she found she was unable even to eat fish for the cold, alien things had also had faces and reproachful eyes. 'You can't feel sorry for a *haddock*,' her husband had said to her. 'Haddocks don't have mothers and children.' Lou had not denied this although she knew it to be untrue, for how else would the haddock have come to exist, but had tried to explain that she could not bring herself to show such disrespect to a once-living creature: could not cook it in hot butter and sprinkle it with parsley and then eat it. 'You cook it for *me*,' said her husband, 'so you know it's dead already so why can't you eat it?' Lou could not answer this without sounding critical of her husband's habits and as they were both aware of it conversation languished. Lou could not bear to hurt anyone's feelings, let alone her husband's, and he was still too newly married to express his feelings freely.

After a while as the marriage grew older he became less meticulous in this respect. Sometimes he called his wife Rabbit, which was wounding: she would not have minded if he had called her Bunny, a nickname with affectionate connotations, but Rabbit was neither fond nor euphonious. Nobody loved a Rabbit. 'Greens and beans and lentils,' he would grumble at her. 'Greens and beans and lentils and lettuce.' One day he made her cry and so had to apologize, which irritated him further when he thought about it. Lou, trying to be accommodating, would occasionally attempt to eat a fishfinger but she didn't like them at all. She told herself that the fish was now so far removed from its face that it should be possible to forget that it had ever had one, but the texture revolted her. He watched her chewing away at a fishfinger one evening and suddenly leaned across and struck her on the arm so that her fork flew to the floor and he had to apologize again. He said that she sometimes seemed so pure that she made him feel almost gross by contrast. The memory of this admission kept returning to annoy him and there was no way he could retract it.

After nine months Lou had a child. As soon as it was born it opened its mouth and howled and kept on howling. Lou spent all her nights walking up and down with it, trying to prevent it from disturbing its father. 'Just leave it to cry,' he said. 'It's good for its lungs.' He felt that he could probably have slept through the noise, but the form of his sweet wife gliding to and fro going 'sh' was a mute, inadvertent reproach that rendered him insomniac. Lou was exhausted. He hadn't been aware of her tiredness until he came home one evening to find the baby crimson with grief and rage and incredulity, lying hiccuping in its pram, and its mother nowhere near. Lou was asleep with her head on the kitchen table and he wondered for a moment whether a marauder had come in the afternoon and killed her. She lived, as he discovered when he touched her, but it was now clear that she would need some help, if only in the day-to-day running of the household. So he rang her mother. If in his voice there was just a hint of the dissatisfied customer, she did not remark it but grew flustered and apologetic because her own husband wasn't very well and could not be left. 'Milly,' she said in a note of inspiration. Milly was between jobs again and for once in her life should be prevailed upon to do something to help the family.

All her life Milly had bitterly resented this sort of imposition on her time and independence: as a child she had never considered it to be her turn to do the washing up or seen it as just that she should help with the shopping. It was her view that since she had not personally chosen to cook meals and soil dishes or supply the household with goods then she should not be expected to involve herself in such matters. As she neared her second decade she had naturally begun to realize that there was a flaw in her reasoning, but it had not lessened her resentment.

She arrived on the afternoon train in a temper and immediately diagnosed her sister as insane. 'You're absolutely mad,' she said, for Lou had volunteered to look after the two small children of a neighbour and was wearily mopping jammy crumbs off the kitchen table while her own baby sat astride her hip, hanging on to her hair. She explained that her neighbour had needed a break and had gone to town to buy a new frock. The pleasure the neighbour had gained from her excursion was clouded when Milly returned her children saying that kind Lou would not be undertaking any more good works for a considerable time. She wondered how it could be that kind Lou had such a witch for a sister.

Milly came back, seized the baby and put it into its pram. She wheeled it out into the garden and told it to look up at the leaves as babies were supposed to do. This early memory would stand it in good stead when it came to write its autobiography. After a moment the baby saw the sense in this and lay gazing upwards, sucking its thumb.

Nor was Milly prepared to stand any nonsense from its father. He was late arriving home so she and Lou had their supper and when he finally appeared she told him that the fridge stood to the left and the stove was just opposite, in case he hadn't noticed, and he could do what he liked. She and Lou were having an early night.

Lou began to sweat with a kind of terror, as one who witnesses the destruction of order, a blasphemy. However, her husband took it calmly enough, merely remarking to Lou, *sotto voce*, that her sister needed tying to a long pole and dipping in a nearby stream.

As the days passed he hardly raised his voice once, and Lou noticed bewilderedly that he had been looking strained and now was not. He began to play with the baby. And the baby, who was now sustained with milk from a bottle and bits of adults' food, sieved, began to sleep through the night and laugh.

Having put things to rights, Milly said she must leave and offered her sister a few words of advice. 'Stand up to them,' she said. 'You're too soft.' And she added something that sounded to Lou like 'and dangerous'. But Lou had been thinking this for quite some time now and had perhaps said it to herself.

'Don't talk to strangers,' repeated Milly as she closed the garden gate, seeing that Lou hadn't heard her the first time. It was the usual family farewell, preferable to 'See you soon' or 'Take care', or any of the other final phrases. Lou was getting more and more vague and dreamy, reflected Milly. The expected response was 'And you', after which no more needed to be said.

'Goodbye,' called Lou, against all the rules. 'Give my love to everyone – and thank you . . .' She went back into the house and stared in the hall mirror at this dangerous person who angered and weakened her loved ones and gave them milk and soft words, when clearly they needed stronger fare. She could see how pretty she was, how pale and golden – like the princess in the fairy story, or the virgin in the picture – and knew herself to be totally unsatisfactory, a snare and a delusion.

After a minute, tired of her own image, she went and looked in the fridge, for her husband would still need to eat no matter how much her care exasperated him. She took out four lamb chops and laid them on the chopping board. None of her knives was very sharp and it took her some time to cut the flesh away from the bone. All the while she thought of lambs gambolling in green fields, of the way they ran and leapt all together and their waggling tails, their faces. But she didn't cry for there seemed no point. She cut the meat into pieces and minced it, rehearsing the evening's conversation, such as it would be.

'What's for supper?' her husband would ask.

'Shepherd's pie,' she would respond.

'Got a shepherd coming, have we?' he would say in what passed for good humour. The thought of the immediate future frightened her more than the prospect of the grave. She began to fry the meat, not finding the smell savoury at all. Everything was dark and the green field only a reflection of the bone-yard.

'All flesh is grass,' she remarked to the baby, wondering whether she should apologize for bringing it into this world of empty promise and mortality. 'I suppose I'm only a little overtired,' she told it earnestly, but within the year she was pregnant again.

AN IDEAL HOME

She went out very seldom and she was drinking too much. The classic image of the deserted wife. She was perfectly aware of what she was doing and she didn't care. Even the rows of empty bottles had ceased to alarm her and she no longer bothered to go to different off-licences to buy drink. She got everything at the Greek shop a street away and brought it back up in the lift in her wheeled shopping basket, not minding in the least what anyone thought. It was a deserted wives' district. Some drank in the pubs, but most drank at home. Occasionally two or three would meet for lunch but they ate hardly anything. They would have champagne cocktails and laugh bitterly about their husbands and their circumstances and then they would go to their separate flats and go on drinking, alone.

After one of these lunches Margaret always felt better. She was quite as unhappy and would get just as drunk as her friends but her case was slightly different. Most of the others had been deserted in favour of younger women. They were racked with jealousy and insecurity about themselves and their ability to attract sexual attention, and would flirt with the waiters until the cocktails made them aggressive, when they would criticize the waiters and sometimes even abuse them for their faulty service. Because waiters were men too. Treacherous and stupid and useless.

Margaret's husband hadn't left her for another woman. He

had one now, but she wasn't the reason he had left. He had told Margaret that he loved her but that she didn't love him; that what she wanted from him was not love; that from the beginning she had been aloof, as though there was a wall around her. He had tried and tried to break through, he said. But she wouldn't let him get close to her and he was too tired to try any more.

She hadn't understood what he was talking about. She loved him to the exclusion of all else and life without him was meaningless. She had given him everything. All her time and her thought had been dedicated to looking after him. The flat was perfect – the chairs upholstered in white tweed were spotless, the cream walls unblemished, the glass dining table glittered above the pale green carpet. The bedroom smelt freshly of lavender and clean linen and nothing was ever left lying around. Even now, when he had gone and she was so often drunk, she kept the place immaculate in case he should come back.

Sometimes she felt certain that he was coming back, a great conviction that he was even now on his way. She would look around her flawless room to make sure that it was quite unmarred. She would rinse out the empty bottles and line them up neatly by the door until the man came to take away the garbage. She would bath and put on a clean nightgown, determined never to let herself go like the other women whose men had left because they no longer loved them.

I am loved, Margaret assured herself; and she felt no jealousy of her husband's mistress. She even felt a faint compassion for her because she knew that no one else would ever reach her own standards of domestic perfection and it could only be a matter of time before her husband realized this and hastened back. Then when she was sober again, she would wonder in bewilderment why he had left her. It was at these moments of anxious sobriety that she felt most desperately lonely. One night she woke up in the small hours with a sudden terrible feeling that her husband had been afraid of her. She blamed the drink for that and changed from gin to vodka.

One day in mid September, returning from lunch with yet another hag-ridden divorcee, Margaret caught sight of her reflection in the wide glass doors to the balcony. How slim she was, how unbowed and unlined and how she suited the stylish room. She poured herself a vodka as a reward and crossed to the glass doors to look out over the city. A perfect woman in a perfect setting. She was finishing her drink when she noticed something misting the glass and put out her hand, blinking, to brush it away. It didn't move, so, concluded Margaret with inebriate clarity, it was on the other side. She put her glass down and inspected it more closely, stepping back, revolted, as she realized it was a spider's web. She put her mind to the problem. She could slide the doors right back and break it and then sweep up the severed strands with her dustpan and brush. She would do that in a minute when she felt steadier, and she poured herself a little more vodka in preparation.

It was a very large web, stretching from the steel jamb of the door to the balcony rail, secured at each side by several cables. It was perfect. It gleamed in the late afternoon sun, a web of picture-book correctness and exactitude. An ideal home, thought Margaret, as she planned its destruction. She jumped as the spider suddenly emerged from its hiding-place between the steel support and the glass and swung down a cable to the centre of the web. It was the biggest spider she had ever seen; grey, with a cream stripe down its back, and legs striped horizontally like Belisha beacons, in cream and grey. Stylish, thought Margaret, approving its deft economy of movement before she remembered to detest it. She stared more closely at what she thought must be its head, until it ejected a stream of white stuff. It's been sick, she thought with unexpected compassion, and then realized she was looking at the wrong end. 'Well, that's charming,' she said aloud; 'spider poohs on the balcony.' But she smiled at the extraordinariness of it, and stood, watching, for quite ten minutes until she had one more little drink and dozed off on the white sofa.

Next morning she went straight to the balcony doors to see if the spider was still there, fully intending to sweep it and its habitation away. It was hanging, quite still, in the centre of the web. An empty web, Margaret realized, and she began to worry because it had nothing to eat. When she went down to the Greek shop she also bought a tin of sardines and a tin of cat food.

She slid the doors open very carefully, leaving just enough space for her to wriggle out, and using the point of a teaspoon, dropped a piece of sardine on to the web. It went straight through. She practised for some time until she got the knack of using her fingers, and flicking a tiny bit at such an angle that it adhered. Then she went back to her own side of the glass to see what would happen. The spider ran down the web to the sardine, picked it up with a few of its legs and ran back to the centre of the web, whereupon it produced some more strands and swiftly and neatly lashed them round its find, just like a man in the food hall at Harrods. Margaret was enchanted and when the spider ate her gift all up she was as gratified as if he'd been an ambassador whom she'd asked to dinner.

Next day the spider caught a few flies and Margaret felt rather annoyed and rejected. Partly because she'd thought there were no flies on her balcony, and partly resenting this evidence of independence.

It rained heavily that night with distant thunder rumbling like a vast stomach and Margaret was surprised to see in the morning that half the web had disappeared, imagining that nature would have been better organized – that spiders would know how to build webs resistant to rain, or that rain would know better than to ruin such an age-old construction. The spider was still there, however, huddled between the steel and the glass and when she looked again the web was once more complete. Margaret was sorry she hadn't watched the repairs in progress and took a light chrome chair to the balcony doors so she could watch everything the spider was up to. She wanted to see what it did with its empty flies, whether it stacked them neatly, as she did her empty bottles, or whether it just flung them idly to the ground like some old drunk. It seemed to matter.

Every day she fed the spider on cat food and sardines. Breakfast, lunch and dinner. No other spider in London, she thought, was as well cared for. She turned down her friends' invitations to lunch and more or less lived on the sardines the spider didn't need.

One afternoon when they had both lunched and she had had her nap, she looked in vain for the spider. It wasn't in the web or on the glass. She called through the open door – spider, spider; but the web hung empty in the autumn sunlight.

Margaret began to cry. She had never felt so lonely. She sat down on her chair and wept for betrayal and emptiness. After a while she dried her eyes and thought of vodka, getting to her feet. Something stirred to the left of them; something was emerging from under the heavy curtains drawn to the side of the balcony doors. Margaret screamed quite loudly and trod on it. It made the only stain on her wide green carpet.

THE BOY WHO SOMETIMES DID
HIS HOMEWORK

Once upon a time there were three sisters. They were not
princesses, but they were sadly spoiled, for their father was
rich. He dealt in Property Speculation and spent most of his
time in the City eating and drinking with his friends and
business associates, none of whom liked him very much. This
was sad but he didn't care, since being rich was his favourite
thing. Because he ate and drank such a lot he grew fat and
instead of going home to his wife and daughters he used to jog
round the City in the dark of the night when his friends and
business associates had gone to bed. Some of his friends and
business associates, before they lay down, would tell their
wives that he was a hard man and some of them would
explain to their children what Property Speculation meant, but
most of them would just go straight to sleep. Sometimes in the
morning the children who didn't know would ask, 'Daddy,
Daddy, what's Property Speculation?' and their fathers would
say, 'I'm in a hurry. Ask your mother,' and leave for the City.
Then the children would lose interest and ask their mothers
what they were going to have for tea. Children mostly have to
work out things like Property Speculation for themselves as
they grow up.

The three sisters were growing up. Not very fast, for childhood takes a long time, far longer than growing old, but every
day they wondered what was going to happen tomorrow and
every day they were disappointed because they had been so

spoiled. They had nothing to look forward to, for their father had given them everything he thought their hearts could desire and would keep them quiet.

Then one morning, very early, in the middle of the winter, their mother gave birth to a baby boy. The sisters had seen even less of their mother than of their father since she took a great interest in Politics and travelled the country talking about it. This was one of the reasons why their father spent the night jogging round the City. He was bored by Politics and preferred money. The sisters went to look at the baby when they felt they had a moment to spare. The oldest, Rose, said he looked red. The second, Lily, said he looked small and the youngest, Daisy, said she didn't like the look of him at all and suggested he be returned to the shop. She didn't know that there was anything that couldn't be bought or sold or sent back if you weren't satisfied with it. Their mother yawned and handed the baby to the latest au pair girl and the sisters went out into the garden where they sat under a lilac tree looking discontented.

Their father drove home from the City. It was too far to jog but he left the car inside the enormous iron gates and trotted up the drive, puffing and panting. He stopped when he saw his daughters. They stared back at him, wondering what he had brought them. 'What have you brought us, Father?' they asked.

'I haven't brought you anything,' he said, adding unwisely that they could think of the baby as one of their Christmas presents. He meant by this to make them feel kindly about the baby but it didn't work. They only liked bought things. 'I brought this for the baby,' he said and he held up a great big box with a toy car in it. None of the girls wanted this car but they were cross that it was a present for the baby and not for them. They began to complain.

'Oh, *honestly*,' said Rose.

'Oh, *really*,' said Lily.

'You're so *mean*,' wailed Daisy.

Fearing that they would go on complaining, for he knew that they could keep it up for days, their father promised that he would immediately buy them each a present and they should have chocolate for breakfast. Half a pound each of the very best chocolate. He always gave them identical amounts in case one should cry, 'It isn't *fair*.'

'What will you buy us?' they asked.

'Wait and see,' he said, wondering what it should be. They already had everything that girls could have. They had dressing-tables and dolls and dresses and ponies and bows to put in their hair. They had rings and books and television sets and videos. They had scent and dolls' houses and mountain bikes. They had potted plants and an ant farm. They had curtains and carpets and lampshades and pictures of pop stars and encyclopedias to improve their minds. They had absolutely everything except kittens. So their father rang up a man he knew and ordered three. He insisted on having the rarest and the most expensive and demanded that they be sent round at once. A small part of his mind that wasn't thinking about Property Speculation was thinking that his daughters might be jealous because their mother had a baby. He thought that if they each had a kitten they might all be happy and never complain again. But mostly he was thinking about Property Speculation.

Christmas came and went and now the girls had more things, as well as the kittens. They had fur coats and Rolex watches and dolls that said 'Mama' and crystal trays to put on their dressing-tables. But as they had presents nearly every day Christmas didn't seem different from any other time and they scowled all through dinner because they didn't like turkey. They had strawberries and peaches and fat grapes, and they didn't think for a moment that this was strange in the middle of winter for they were spoiled. They made their father turn up the central heating and draw the curtains and it could have been the middle of summer. Their mother wore a big blue hat and their father smoked a big cigar and the baby lay in his cradle until the au pair girl gave him his bottle. Their mother talked about Politics and their father talked about Property Speculation but they didn't talk to each other and they didn't talk to the girls. They talked to themselves. Then Father went jogging and Mother went to a cocktail party to tell her Member of Parliament what he should do next. The au pair girl gave the kittens their milk and opened a tin of chicken bits for them, and the sisters lay on the sofa and watched a television film about very rich people on a tropical island.

'Oh how I wish I lived on a tropical island,' said Rose and Lily and Daisy. 'Just look at those lucky people. They have everything they want and it never rains and the wind never blows.' If they had read their encyclopedias they would have known that they were quite mistaken and that tropical islands could be uncomfortable, but they were too lazy to read. They lay there, eating chocolates and feeling envious and disagreeable and after a while they felt sick.

So the years went by and the kittens grew into cats and the baby grew into a little boy. He climbed trees and ate the apples, he rolled down the slope of the lawn and ate the blackberries that grew at the bottom.

'You are disgusting,' said his sisters. 'Your face is all covered in juice.' He made friends with the gardener's boy, and sometimes he did his homework and sometimes he didn't. He played with the cats under the lilac tree until his sisters noticed and told him not to. They said they were *their* cats. The boy thought this was silly and went on playing with them. So the girls made their father buy golden collars and leads and they kept their cats chained to them.

For a while the cats protested. They squirmed and they jumped and they scratched and they yowled *Miawoooo*. Being such rare and unusual cats they had strange and piercing voices and they nearly drove the sisters mad. Rose and Lily and Daisy got down on their knees and looked into the long, slanting, angry eyes of their cats. 'Don't you realize, you stupid cats,' they said, 'that you are highly privileged to wear golden collars and have an au pair girl to give you chicken bits out of a tin? Don't you understand how lucky you are to belong to *us*?' The cats lay flat on the ground and stared back, their tails twitching. 'And what's more,' said the sisters, 'if you don't behave we'll ring up a man our father knows who will have you made into fur muffs, for it sometimes gets very cold round here.' The cats spat a little and then they sulked but they put their heads into the golden collars and let the sisters lead them round. 'Talking of cold,' said Rose, who rather resembled her mother, 'I think we should get Father to do something about it.'

'I do so agree,' said Lily. 'It's ridiculous that people in our position should have to put up with it.'

'Changing it would cost a great deal of money,' said Daisy, who took after her father.

'That is what money is *for*,' said her sisters. 'To change things. We'll speak to Father when he jogs home.'

Some days later when their father returned from the City the sisters spoke to him. 'Father,' they said, 'we want to have a few words with you.' Their father trembled, for a few words from his daughters always meant trouble. He wished he'd stayed in the City. 'We want you to change things,' they said, 'so that there will be no more change. Frequent change,' they went on, 'means inconvenience and discomfort. We do not like spring for it is damp and often windy. Summer is tolerable but it is not to be relied upon for sometimes it, too, is damp and windy. Autumn is usually damp and windy and winter is not tolerable at all since it is always damp and windy. We want conditions to be perfect at all times. We are not satisfied.'

So their father arranged, at enormous expense, to have the garden heated. He put a tall fence all round it and bought trees that never lost their leaves. Where there were barren patches he put plastic trees that looked even more real than real trees. He put a glass roof all over the garden so the rain and the snow and the wind never came through. And the garden stayed the same all the year round.

'That's better,' said the girls, and for a while, as long as their father remembered to bring them presents, they were quite pleased. Now the cats, on the other hand, were not pleased, for cats, although they like warmth sometimes, do not like it all the time. They like to know when the cold is coming, they can smell cold from where it begins in the icy Arctic wastes, and when it comes closer their fur stands up on end and their eyes sparkle like icicles: their tails wave and they begin to run and skitter. They run up trees for no reason that humans can see, and they grow young again with excitement and they play and play. So when there was no more cold they grew bored and they began to grow old.

'Some creatures are *never* satisfied,' said the sisters crossly. 'Some creatures are hopelessly ungrateful. Just look at those tiresome cats.' The cats miaowed sadly and sullenly, and they looked longingly up at the top of the fence and the glass roof. 'If they're going to behave like *that*,' said the sisters, 'we'd better get rid of them for they will only make us feel unhappy.' Besides, they didn't want to see anything growing old for that was a change and they hated change. 'We'll tell the gardener's boy to take them away,' they said, 'and our father can buy us something nicer instead.'

The boy, who had been carrying on like boys do, climbing the trees and eating the plums, rolling in the grass and playing with his toy car, and sometimes doing his homework and sometimes not, hadn't really noticed that it was now always summer until one day he wondered when it was going to be Christmas. He went and asked the gardener's boy who was carrying a sack. 'When is it going to be Christmas,' he asked, 'and what have you got in that sack?'

'In three days' time,' said the gardener's boy, 'and I have a sack full of three cats which I am taking somewhere where your sisters won't see them, for their whiskers are going grey and they go miaow sorrowfully in the night.'

'Then it should be snowing,' said the boy, 'for sometimes I do my homework and I have learned that it always snows at Christmas. And if my sisters no longer want the cats they shall be mine.'

'There is a roof over the garden,' said the gardener's boy, 'and the snow can't come in.'

'Then I shall break it,' said the boy and he did. He climbed the tallest tree, followed by the cats, who were feeling younger already, and he poked it with a stick until it broke and shattered, and as it fell it turned to ice. It lay as frost all over the trees and the lawns, and it glittered in the evening sunlight.

'According to my homework,' said the boy, 'at Christmas-time there is sometimes a wind from the icy Arctic wastes.'

'There is a fence round the garden,' said the gardener's boy, 'and the wind can't come in.'

'Then I shall pull it down,' said the boy and he did. He dug away at the bottom of it, and the cats, who were feeling younger all the time, dug too. It fell and turned into brown reeds and the wind from the icy Arctic wastes blew among them and the cats played with it.

'Your sisters are going to be hopping mad,' said the gardener's boy, 'and I don't know what your father's going to say when he jogs home,' but the boy wasn't listening. He was looking at the garden all ready for Christmas.

The sisters, who were in the house eating marzipan and playing Monopoly, didn't notice that things had changed until the cats came racing through with their fur standing on end and their eyes shining like the stars that were now visible in the sky. The sisters looked through the windows and saw the moon rising so that the garden under a fall of snow gleamed like glory. They saw their father walking home, not jogging, for the bottom had fallen out of Property Speculation, which is a thing that happens sometimes, and he wasn't rich any more. He went and told their mother who took her hat off and said, 'Well, never mind. The girls and I can take in washing and the boy can help the gardener's boy grow vegetables.' She was a sensible woman at heart and had immediately seen the advantages of having a real garden in which to grow potatoes and cabbages instead of a pretend one.

I cannot say that the girls were at first pleased with the change in their fortunes but there was nothing they could do about it and on Christmas day they had to admit that the garden looked pretty, all silver and white. They picked dark green holly with scarlet berries and they all gave each other things that their father had given them and they had forgotten about. Some of the things had never been taken out of their boxes so they were a nice surprise. There was enough for everyone and they gave the gardener's boy their ponies and they gave the au pair girl some of their dresses and a pink television set that didn't work, for they were yet to learn about *real* kindness.

Their father lost a lot of weight and his friends and business associates stopped calling him a hard man and their mother gave up Politics, which saved her a lot of time. When the spring came again the girls looked younger, like the cats, and Rose planted roses and Lily planted lilies and Daisy frolicked all over the lawn. The cats played in the fallen leaves in the dark corners of the shrubbery and the boy lay on his back looking up at the huge sky, chewing a stalk of grass, and sometimes he did his homework and sometimes he didn't.

RATS AND RABBITS

She said, 'There are rats in the bank behind the chickens', and he said, 'No, there're not. I've never seen them.'

Dorothy had seen them – seen their quick brown backsides hastening under the overhanging grass into holes in the bank, just perceptible on the perimeter of sight when she went out to shake the tablecloth: cunning.

'Horrible things,' she said.

'You need glasses,' he said. 'There's no rats.'

She closed her teeth tightly and lifted his cap from the table to hang it behind the door where it should be. She wrung out the dishcloth and carefully wiped the table for the second time since he'd come in from the fields. It seemed he was determined to deny the existence of rats, as he denied the existence of germs or mad axemen. He was fearless – as well he might be: he was built like a barn and was never ill. Dorothy wasn't a particularly nervous woman, but she disliked the idea of rats. The thought of their proximity made her uneasy, like the thought of fault in herself.

'They carry disease,' she said.

'There's no rats,' he repeated.

She wished he would go and look. Take his gun and a big stick and scour the bank – not now so much because she was afraid, but to show some belief in her. When he left her alone in the evenings she wasn't really afraid, but all the same he shouldn't do it.

He said, 'Another cup of tea.'

She picked up the pot from the table in front of him, added milk and a lot of sugar, and stirred it. He said the tea was cold and she replied that it had been hot when she made it.

For a while he read the local paper, very loudly, with breathings and rustlings, and she took his boots from where they stood, empty of him, on her shining lino, and put them outside the kitchen door, banging them against the wall to dislodge some of the mud that had come with him from the fields. It fell on the clean flags and she took her broom and swept it on to the garden – her garden. His was to the left where his mother had planted it – a vegetable garden laid in rows which he tended in the evening before the light failed.

She tended her garden by day, putting eggshells and tea leaves round the roots of the roses. He laughed at her for a townie and said why not face-tissues and her old nylons? She would tell him in the longest words she could call to mind that it was scientific, what she did: that her roses needed calcium and tannin to grown up big and strong. She bought a paperback on herb lore and told him everything a countryman ought to know about parsley and basil and rue. He would laugh for quite a minute at a time, so as not to hear her long words and her wise saws.

Once a month he emptied the privy on his vegetable garden. Dorothy was aware that he was waiting for her to express disgust; but she knew that that too was scientific, and nothing would bring her to express the disgust which, in truth, she felt.

She said, 'Roy.'

He grunted, but not in answer, merely as a preliminary to asking her why she'd put his boots away when he had to go back to the fields to see to the sheep.

'Cut the young rams today,' he said. 'Don't want them in the long grass.'

Dorothy said nothing. He had never burdened her with the details of these crude operations – not, she felt, from sensitivity, but from lack of it. He simply didn't understand how deeply he could have upset her, how he could have teased and tormented her with tales of conception, castration and all the shepherd's and the sheep's daily tribulations.

At first, in the springtime, he had asked her to help him pull lambs; but when she learned that this meant from the body of the mother, she had declined. She would help him round up the sheep when the old dog wouldn't work, she would walk over the hills after strays in the dusk; but she would not be present at the more important moments of their short sheep lives – although she would always agree to hand-rear the rejected or weakly lambs.

She said, 'Roy, I won't feed the chickens until you dig out those rats.'

'There aren't any rats,' he said, as he closed the door behind him.

She wiped the table again, very carefully, and washed his mug and plate. He was to have cod for his dinner, with frozen peas from the supermarket in town. Dorothy never wasted the vegetables that he grew. She used some herself, but most she gave to his sister-in-law who lived near by and had four little children. Roy knew that Dorothy was good-hearted, but he also knew that that wasn't the reason.

He stopped on the field above where the chickens ran and looked down at the cottage and Dorothy's garden. She kept them very neat. He called once, 'Dorothy', perhaps to rebuke her for supposing there to be rats in the field, perhaps to praise her for the evening sky, which was just beginning to glow like an eggshell lit by candle flame.

She had told him when he first brought her here that it was a beautiful place, and he had been grateful to her for taking so much pleasure. Once he had watched her watching an old fox walking in the winter sunlight the whole breadth of the snow-covered meadow on the other side of the valley, and something in the quality of that watching intensity had made him think of his mother when the baby was going to sleep.

She thought she heard him call, but the tap was running and perhaps she was mistaken. She went round the side of the cottage and looked up at the field but he was away, striding over the lip of the hill.

The kitchen seemed suddenly very light as it grew darker outside. It was time to lock up the chickens, but she thought she would peel the potatoes and boil them and the peas; and even fry the cod – they would keep warm in the oven. He wouldn't eat any of her fancy sauces. Once she had teased him with blithe thoughtlessness, saying that some nice sauce would help make his peas stick to his knife, and he had looked at her for a long time before he said, 'You think I'm ignorant, don't you?'

That was a word she never used now. Just the thought of it burned her tongue. They had had their disagreements. Once she had lain all day in the garden in the sun wearing only her bra and knickers and he had told her that his mother had never had a holiday, had brought up seven children in that house and had still found time to make her own clothes.

That was easy to see, Dorothy had said, cross from too much sun – judging from the photographs. Insulting his mother, his very blood. She had made him buy new clothes for himself, and have his hair cut regularly; but it didn't feel to him so much like care, but more like shame. He was always irritable when he wore his new suit.

There had been raised voices, a raised saucepan once. Her wedding ring had flown, twinkling, the length of the kitchen, but they had both searched for it; and now anger was seldom overt.

146

Dorothy knew she must do something about the chickens. She remembered the quick whisk of brown rump and wondered if perhaps she really was afraid: rats, toothed and tailed, with little naked human hands. But these are only country rats, she told herself, because now she wanted to lock up the chickens. A dog ferret had got among them at the turn of the year and killed three before Roy killed him with two great hammer blows on his flat snake skull. Dorothy, screaming, had fled with her hands over her eyes and her thumbs in her ears from the welter of feather and fur and blood. She had never known such violence, such screeching and clucking, such noise of boot into bucket, of claw on concrete and Roy grunting. He often grunted, she thought – at varying moments – and she flushed, alone in her clean kitchen.

She got the big torch from the outhouse, although it wasn't dark at all yet, and pulled on her wellingtons. There was her smart red mac hanging behind the door, but she seldom wore it now. The women round about wore quilted anoraks, and she didn't think anyone realized how smart her mac was, although Roy had once said it was a pretty colour.

The garden was beginning to smell of her night-scented stock coming into its own, and the whole valley lay at her feet like a soup plate of salad, losing colour as the evening drew on. She said in her head to her old friends who had told her she was mad to uproot herself at her age and go off to live in the sticks with a man she hardly knew, that none of them had ever known a place as beautiful as this.

Defiantly she turned her torch to light her under the shadow of the house.

Roy came back late. She knew there was something wrong by the speed of his feet on the flags, and she got up to face the wrong at once.

He came in very quickly, carrying his cap upside down, and

he spoke. 'There's your rats,' he said, emptying his cap on the kitchen table.

Little baby rabbits fell out. Dead ones. About six of them, as far as she could see.

'There's your rats,' he said again, and the tears were pouring down his face.

LAST LAUGH

I was sitting in the pub one morning drinking Guinness and wondering if the lunch had started burning yet, when I began overhearing one of those conversations to which you fear you'll never hear the conclusion. The speaker will let her voice fade to a whisper or turn away, or the person you're with will suddenly feel the need to describe last night's dream to you. Someone in a vest and tattooed upper arms will put on some loud music or the pub will fill up with chatterers. I once read a murder story and found too late that the last pages were missing. I'd already guessed who dunnit but it wasn't the same and the experience still rankles. 'Listen,' I said to the person I was with, 'I want you to go and buy a newspaper and two more Guinnesses and then I don't want you to say a word until I say you can.' Then I edged my chair towards the table behind me and listened intently. I had heard a woman say, 'Did I ever tell you about the time I tried out some do-it-yourself marriage guidance?' She was slightly drunk and had just accepted another gin and tonic so I hoped she'd be able to tell her tale coherently. Someone else muttered something and she went on.

'It was when I was living across the river. Denis had left already so I was on my own but I was doing alright. I'd got to know some of the neighbours, through the school run mostly, and all the kids knew each other so there was quite a bit of social intercourse in one way and another. Anyway, after a while I noticed one of the neighbours getting thinner and rather too enthusiastic, if you know what I mean. She was having her hair done in different ways and she'd bought some sandals with straps that do right up to the knee – you know the sort of thing – and dangly earrings and a frock with a tight belt. And the kids were looking the way kids do when mummy's attention is wandering. One in particular. She was my daughter's best friend and she'd taken to stealing things. Just little things, some beads, and biscuits from the kitchen cupboard, but it was annoying. I couldn't say much. You know how you can't. And all the time the neighbour was getting more and more indiscreet. I'd never known her all that well. She was married to some chap in the City and to be absolutely honest I'd always found them a bit boring. OK to talk to if you met them in the street or the school concert when you'd talk to anybody, but if you found yourself sitting next to them at dinner you'd remind yourself to think twice before accepting an invitation to that house again. I mean they'd go to the opera which is alright if you like that sort of thing, but they wouldn't leave it at that – they'd tell you about it. Especially her. Come to think of it I'd never exchanged more than a dozen words with him.

'Then one morning I met her in the chemist's and she told me all about it. She'd got to the stage where she had to tell somebody. She'd have told the chemist if there'd been no one else in the shop. She was in love. Well I knew that. I should think the whole street knew it. He was a social worker or trades unionist or something. God knows where she'd found him but he'd opened up a whole new world for her, she felt completely alive for the first time in her life. You know the sort of thing. It was rather touching really. A bit like the children when they see a rhinoceros or something for the first time and they can't believe anyone's ever seen one before or can understand how amazing it is. And not a word about the opera. I felt awfully sorry for her. I could see where it was all going. She said her husband was being understanding. Oh dear. She said the children were being a bit difficult but they'd come round. She said she knew it was all going to be alright. I couldn't say much, could I? I couldn't say there was no way it was going to be alright. She wouldn't have believed me, would she? Oh, OK, just a small one. G and T.'

Here there was a pause as someone went to get another lot of drinks. I didn't dare turn round for a furtive look in case they noticed me and realized I could hear every word. I'd been very lucky in choosing this pub on a Sunday morning for it was still almost empty and my companion was happily reading the paper. I was making my Guinness last.

'So where was I?' she continued when she had a fresh gin and tonic. 'Oh yes. Well it was getting towards the summer hols and I hadn't seen her for some time. Her little girl was being a pain so I knew things weren't going too well but I wasn't all that interested. Then one evening she rang up. She was sobbing her heart out so I told her to have a stiff drink and I'd be right over. She was sitting in the kitchen looking like the wrath of God, swollen eyes and red in the face and her husband was floating about in the background, just looking embarrassed. He was obviously a good man. He hadn't thumped her or anything. So I said, "What's the matter?" and she said her lover had left her and she started to cry again. So I told her to cheer up and look on the bright side and think how lucky she was to have such a lovely home and such a good husband. The house was all done up in stripped pine and bamboo and mirrors with writing on, but it was no time to be concerned with the truth. "Just think," I said, "of the lovely man you're married to and your lovely children." I'd accepted a couple of drinks by then. I said the social worker had clearly been a chancer and a thoroughly bad thing and she was well rid of him and I wished I had a heavenly husband like hers. So after a while she managed a little smile and I said I'd be going now and I finished my drink . . . Oh alright. Here, let me. Yes, just a small G and T. Thanks.'

By now I could have done with another Guinness but I still didn't dare move so I sat there looking at a picture of somebody drinking something. It was trying to be an old-fashioned pub.

'So I got up to leave,' said the woman behind me, 'and he said he'd see me home. I thought it was a bit rum because it's all of three paces from their house to mine, but I said to myself perhaps it was just that he was a gentleman. And I opened my door and reached for the light switch and there he was right behind me. Really no gentleman. You see, what had happened was that he'd been listening to me singing his praises. He wasn't to know I'd been making it all up as I went along. He thought I meant it and it would've been a bit awkward to explain. You see how I couldn't. Can't you? Can't you see how I couldn't? How I couldn't possibly explain?'

She was obviously suffering from some residual guilt and her friend grunted something soothing.

'Well one thing led to another and I began to see him quite often. He was really rather sweet when he didn't go to the opera and he was making quite a lot of money and I was beginning to think I could do worse. She, of course, had gone back to the social worker. You know how these things never do just end like that. It had been a lovers' tiff and it had blown over and doubtless there'd be many more tiffs before it finally blew out. So things were just idling along when one day she suddenly rang up in tears again. She'd got reason to suspect that her husband was having an affair. This had brought her to her senses. She now knew where her loyalties lay etc. and she was giving up the social worker and she was really going to work at her marriage. I never did know what that meant, did you? How do you work at a marriage? Either it works or it doesn't. Anyway that was what she was going to do. So, of course, I backed out. I was a tiny bit annoyed because I'd begun to get used to her husband. We used to meet in secret and eat oysters and drink champagne. I told you he was doing well in the City, didn't I? Still, that was a minor consideration with a family's happiness at stake, I told myself. So I threw him back. And do you know what he did? He didn't go back to his wife. He went off with a girl in his office, half his age ... Yes, I will. Now I come to think of it I'll have a double. They moved away soon after that and I never saw either of them again. I don't know what happened to her ...'

I did of course but I wasn't going to enlighten her. Why should she know the end of the story? I told my companion he could get me another Guinness now. Chancer, indeed. He'd given up social work and we'd started a small business together selling stripped pine and bamboo furniture. And as for children stealing ... *her* daughter had stolen my Indian silk shawl as a present for her mother. She was probably wearing it now but I didn't look round to find out. There was really no point in renewing the acquaintance.

THE TRAVELLER

He had been travelling for what seemed to have been a long, long time: for so long that he could scarcely remember when or where he had begun. He knew he had once been weary but that had passed, and now he felt nothing at all.

There was a sound from somewhere, the sound of metal striking upon metal: a sound that meant the existence of man – a factory, an anvil, a dinner gong or a bell tolling. If he had stood in need of comfort he might have been reassured to know that he was not, after all, alone. If he had been fearful he might have stopped, turned and sought a hiding-place, for the clashing of metal, the manipulation of machinery most frequently signals danger to man: destruction and war, the rending of flesh and the losing of blood. The dark gods had not forgiven man for discovering their cold treasure, but let it go with a curse upon it. He knew that now, as he knew many things. Something not unlike a black dog trailed behind him.

The human soul does not always take easily to separation. The human mind with which it has shared its housing exerts a powerful influence, principally upon that very housing, but also upon that element which it cannot comprehend. It experiences itself as supreme and knows itself to be mortal, reacting with the malignity of all animal kind to a threat to its survival. Often it perceives the soul as traitor, betrayer, knowing, if not believing, that when the soul departs it will leave mind and body alone together, without light, until ... but the mind seldom accepts that 'until'. The word posits a condition which the mind, seeing even through its arrogance its ultimate powerlessness, can only reject. To put it at its simplest – the mind likes to make itself up and is endlessly loath to yield its supremacy. This is because of something that happened in a garden all that long, long time ago.

The mind of the traveller had followed him: it could not have done so without his permission, but now he began to get tired of it as it dragged at his heels, complaining.

'Shut up,' said the traveller. 'I'm trying to see where I'm going.'

'You can't do that without me,' said his mind.

'Yes, I can,' said the traveller.

'How?' inquired his mind, petulantly.

'I don't know,' said the traveller.

'That's because you're not using me,' said his mind, and it whined briefly.

'I don't need you,' said the traveller. 'I can't think why I brought you. You're just a hindrance. If you'd be quiet I could see where I was.'

'You aren't anywhere,' said his mind, 'you're in limbo.'

'That,' said the traveller, 'is not a concept that you were wont to entertain.'

'It's a word like any other,' said his mind, sitting down in the road.

The traveller quickened his step, feeling suddenly freer. Ahead he could see what looked like a gate, and beyond it a slow light rising, silken pale like the light of dawn. Although he had not previously taken account of it, he had been moving, not in the dark, for he had no sense of blackness, but without illumination through a colourless opacity.

'Wait,' said his mind.

'Oh,' said the traveller, forlornly.

'What's wrong?' asked his mind, panting slightly.

'I can't see it now,' said the traveller.

'See what?' asked his mind.

'There was a garden,' said the traveller, 'and there was someone standing there.'

'That would have been the gardener,' said his mind. 'Who did you think it was?'

'I don't know,' said the traveller.

'You don't know anything,' said his mind, and it latched its claws into the hem of his garment and let itself be dragged for a long, long time.

The metallic noise had faded, but now it grew louder again. Louder and louder, so that whichever way the traveller had turned it seemed he would have arrived at its source.

The white ghosts of blossom swayed in the hedgerow and a sudden wind disturbed the stillness. The traveller moved round a long corner and came to a village: there were lamps hanging outside the houses and people stood in the street.

'Careful,' said the dog, 'people, danger . . .'

'I'm inclined to agree with you up to a point,' said the traveller, 'but you, despite your aggressive instincts and over-confident demeanour, have frequently held me back and prevented me from attempting new – possibly enjoyable – adventures and experiences.'

'Ingrate,' snarled the dog, his ears laid flat.

'Down,' said the traveller.

The first people he passed said nothing, but stood watching his approach. The traveller had found this to be usual with all living beings: they wait for one older or wiser, or failing that, one less nervous or possibly more inquisitive, to intercept and question the stranger – the oldest inhabitant, a small child, or the individual who has been marked out as the village idiot. It is best if the young males are employed elsewhere when the stranger arrives, for often they will feel it to be their part to demand of him his money or his life. They will inquire where he has come from and despise him for his alien status, no matter what his answer. Then, in all likelihood, they will kill him and bury his body outside the town boundaries.

'Remember, remember ...' whispered the dog. 'Don't let them see your watch or hear the way you speak.'

Now the traveller stopped in his tracks and turned to address his companion. 'Shut up,' he said. 'I've had enough of you. I will admit that in the past you have been of assistance to me but, on the other hand, your antics have lost me friends and stopped me from seeing over walls because I've been looking down and listening to you. I've realized just now that one of the reasons I no longer need you is because I am no longer afraid.'

'Why not?' demanded the dog craftily.

'I don't know,' said the traveller.

'Of course you don't,' said the dog. 'You know nothing without me.'

A person in a vaguely official-seeming uniform stepped forward and spoke. 'Would you like me to take him now and put him in the pound?' he asked. 'He will be retrained and restored to you in the course of what you still think of as time.'

'What's he talking about?' asked the dog, agitated now. 'What rubbish is this?'

The traveller hesitated. Truth to tell, the dog had succeeded in alarming him slightly and it would seem very strange without him when they had been together and interdependent for so long. The official stepped back, smiling. 'It's all right,' he said, 'you can keep him as long as you wish. We have no hard and fast rules about dogs at this stage. They do no harm here.' His tone was benevolent and held not a hint of rebuke, but the traveller felt again that sense of loss that had assailed him as he neared the garden and his mind had bade him wait. He had that feeling of emptiness and disorientation that comes when you realize that you have made a very great mistake, yet do not quite know just where the error lies.

'Damn dog,' he said, and went on down the village street. A metalworker was hammering away at a copper bowl outside a booth.

'That was the noise you heard,' said the dog.

But the traveller knew it had been a different noise and was overwhelmed by the knowledge of anticlimax. He stopped outside an inn and looked through the windows. It appeared plain but clean inside and he went towards the door. The dog sat down. 'Now what?' asked the traveller.

'If you'd simply look round a bit,' said the dog, 'you'd see a modern hotel across the road. With all its aspects proclaiming comfort and modern convenience. Why are you considering that grotty old pub?' It leapt to its feet and, straining at the leash, dragged him to the splendid portals of a new and gleaming building which, oddly enough, the traveller had previously failed to notice. 'Dogs Welcome' read a placard on the reception desk.

'Name?' asked the clerk, teeth gleaming.

'Christian,' said the traveller, with what was, for him, astonishing promptitude, and the dog nipped him on the ankle.

'Just one moment, sir,' said the clerk smoothly, disappearing through a side door.

'Why did you do that?' demanded the traveller of his dog.

'Why did you say that?' demanded the dog.

'It's the truth,' said Christian. 'I don't like this place. I prefer the inn over the road and I'm going there. Anyway, they won't let me stay here once they see I've got no luggage. I'm not listening to you any more.'

When the clerk returned with the head clerk, whose name was Death, they saw only the swinging doors. 'He's gone to the Traveller's Rest,' said the junior clerk, 'but I daresay he'll be back, and it's not as though we're short of custom. There's been quite a rush recently.'

Death said nothing. He seldom did.

The inn door was open but the inn was empty.

'Is there anybody there?' cried Christian, and he tapped with his knuckles on the bar.

'Some place,' sneered the dog. 'Why should there be anybody here?'

'It's an inn and it's open,' said Christian. 'There will be somebody here.'

'This is new,' said the dog. 'This touching faith.'

'Actually,' said Christian, 'I am using the merest common sense, which you, despite your pretensions, have always signally lacked.' Someone was singing in the back room. 'Hullo,' called Christian. 'Anybody there?'

The innkeeper came through, wearing an expression poised between inquiry and a readiness to be welcoming should the need arise. 'And who have we here?' he said.

'Peculiar sort of innkeeper, talking like that,' said the dog, sniggering. 'He hasn't even asked your name.'

'Why should he?' said Christian.

'The other one did,' said the dog.

'This one asked who I am,' said Christian. 'He asked who I am, not what I'm called.

The innkeeper regarded them amiably as they argued. 'There

164

are kennels out at the back,' he said, 'if he gets obstreperous. Made specially.'

Christian's mind stood on its hind legs and put its front paws on the bar. It stared balefully at the innkeeper and opened its jaws to speak, but, for some reason, under the innkeeper's friendly gaze, it could only achieve an irritated whine.

'Down,' said Christian.

Across the road, in the Hotel Splendide, the manager came forth to greet the latest guest. This guest was surrounded by luggage and was considerably ill-tempered. He had had a confused and unpleasant journey, jostled at the airport by strange hordes of unfamiliar people, troubled at the immigration desk when he couldn't find his passport, and subjected to close and impertinent questioning in Customs. Even now he could not relax, despite the sumptuousness of his surroundings.

'It's not good enough,' he said, for he was a wealthy man and accustomed to deference.

'I am your servant, sir,' said the manager, smoothly, for he had an ancient knowledge of the intricately varied desires and whims of mankind.

'A room,' said the guest, 'a room with a bathroom *en suite* and a view of the ocean.'

'Certainly, sir,' said the manager, and he clapped his hands to summon a minion to guide the guest to his heart's desire. The guest began to feel better.

'Think he'll be staying?' asked Death, *sotto voce*.

'Oh, I think so,' said the manager, glancing appraisingly at the pile of luggage. 'I should definitely think so.'

'You want money in advance?' asked the guest from the foot of the stairs.

'No, no,' said the manager, 'that will not be necessary. Not necessary at all.'

'How coarse,' said a hotel employee, passing by. 'Do you want me to roll out the ocean or will you do it yourself?'

'I'll do it later,' said the manager, who enjoyed exercising his powers. 'He's not going to be noticing the view for a while.' He went to the dining-room, which lay at the back of the hotel, and looked through the windows at the wilderness stretching away to infinity.

'You didn't ask who he is,' said the hotel employee.

'I don't think he knows,' said Death.

The guest sat down on the bed and looked around; his sight was blurred with tiredness and he felt fragmented and unclear. Everything seemed to be all right in the room as far as he could tell, warm and more luxurious than comfortable – which was the way he preferred things to be. He wished he could remember how he had come here, what he was doing here, and why. All through the journey he had been oppressed by the sound of metal striking on metal: he had thought that perhaps the plane was breaking up, or was under attack from terrorists or madmen, but now as he took off his coat he was reassured. After all, it was only the sound of coins, representatives of his riches, falling one upon another in his pockets. He lay down and tried to sleep.

'How long do you think he'll be staying?' asked the head receptionist.

'Well, that rather depends, doesn't it?' said the manager. 'As ever, it all just rather depends . . .'

The guest came down to dinner, still in querulous humour, and gazed around at the dining-room. 'Place is pretty empty tonight,' he observed to a waiter. 'Nobody else staying?'

'Oh yes, sir,' said the waiter, tossing a napkin over his lower arm in that gesture that is at once insolent and obsequious, and warns the more intelligent and discerning diner that he would do well not to order the soup or any dish capable of concealing things unwholesome, for he is not loved and is not truly welcome here.

The guest was blind to such subtleties. 'Bring me a bottle of Château d'Yquem,' he demanded, 'and let me see the menu.'

After a meal consisting of several courses the guest rose, folded his napkin, left the dining-room and went towards the door.

'Have a pleasant evening, sir,' said the manager, creamily.

Apart from a slight raising of the upper lip the guest ignored him. 'I don't like the feller,' he said aloud, as though by way of excuse.

A lady in the doorway responded. 'But he's charming,' she said. The guest gave her a look and pushed by into the street. The manager, laughing, made a note on a memo pad.

The guest crossed over and went into the inn opposite. 'I'll have a brandy and soda,' he said, and looked around for company. His glance fell on Christian, who was sitting at a rough-hewn table with his mind at his feet. 'Nice dog you've got there,' said the guest. 'May I join you?' He wrinkled his forehead as though trying to remember something, and the dog watched interestedly. 'Name's Smith,' he said, at last. 'John Smith. Sir John Smith,' he amended. For all the later years of his life he had known that the knighthood that was rightfully his was withheld because of the envy, spite and all uncharitableness of certain people in positions of power. Now he claimed it without compunction, with pride.

The dog, who had taken him for a commercial traveller, was surprised and then puzzled. It knew the man was lying and yet saw no reason to disbelieve him. Whimpering, it put its head on its paws.

'Christian,' said Christian. 'How do you do.'

'Funny old place,' observed Sir John, gazing round with disfavour. 'Could do with a bit of modernizing. I'm at the hotel over the road. It's not perfect by any means, but it's got everything.'

'Then why isn't it perfect?' asked Christian, because he wanted to know.

'Good question,' said Sir John, taking this in the spirit it was intended.

'Because nothing ever is,' put in the dog, speaking for the first time that evening.

'He's right,' said Sir John, and he sounded relieved. 'The dog's got it. Nothing's ever perfect. Take the meal I had tonight. Perfectly cooked, perfectly served, and now I don't even feel as though I'd eaten at all – can't even remember what I had.'

'Chinese, was it?' inquired the dog.

'No,' said Sir John, 'just your perfectly usual, perfectly sound international cuisine.'

'Christian hates international cuisine,' said the dog. 'We both do, actually. We both prefer dishes indigenous to the country we find ourselves in and, failing that, we like simple things – bread and cheese, vegetables and fish – neither of us can bear pretentiousness in food. We like good honest flavours, simply expressed and undisguised by sauces and dubious provenance . . .'

Christian was ashamed of his dog carrying on in this *bien pensant* fashion. He kicked it. 'Shut up,' he said, 'or I'll lock you in the kennels at the back.' The dog would have bitten him, but Christian was too quick for it and smacked it on the snout. 'Be still,' he ordered.

'Smart dog,' remarked Sir John, but rather coolly, since its speech had rebuked him for his sincerely held views.

'He'll be all right once he's learned his place,' said Christian. 'I get impatient with him but I couldn't really do without him.'

'I'd better get back,' said Sir John, 'check up everything's all right. Place looks secure enough but I've got a lot of very valuable stuff in my luggage, and you never know.'

The dog said in an impartial tone, 'Christian didn't bring any luggage.'

'Travelling light, eh?' said Sir John with a patronizing smile.

'As light as I can,' said Christian.

'I haven't paid yet,' said Sir John as he stood up. 'Innkeeper.'

'On the house,' said the innkeeper.

'That's very civil of you,' said Sir John, delighted at this beneficence. He looked more closely at him and narrowed his eyes. 'Feller looks familiar,' he said to Christian. 'Reminds me of someone.'

'He looks like the desk clerk over the road,' said the dog. 'Almost identical.'

'Probably related,' said Sir John. 'What you doing tomorrow?' he asked Christian.

'I'll probably go on,' said Christian.

'Bit soon, isn't it?' said Sir John. 'I'm going to hang around for a while. I'm tired of travelling.'

'Or I may stay around for a while too,' said Christian, and he shivered.

'Feeling the draught?' asked Sir John. 'You should've brought some warm things.' He thought complacently of his own luggage.

'Goose over my grave,' said Christian. The inn door suddenly swung open and he felt for a moment lost and desolate. 'But I want to get home . . .' he said. The dog whined.

'I'm in no hurry,' said Sir John. 'I'm going to check it out round here before I decide what to do next. Might just settle here. Lot depends on the golf-course.'

'I'll walk across with you,' said Christian, 'and give the dog a bit of an airing.' Outside it was neither light nor dark and there was no wind.

'Pleasant climate,' observed Sir John, '. . . equable.'

'I'd prefer something a bit more bracing, myself,' said the dog, who was seldom satisfied and in the habit of complaining.

'If it's fine tomorrow,' said Sir John, 'I'll take you for a run along the seashore.'

Christian saw that the dog and Sir John had more in common than he would have supposed. 'I'm going to follow the road,' he said. The dog lifted his lip in a sneer, then ran eagerly towards the door of the Hotel Splendide.

'Coming in for a nightcap?' inquired Sir John. The dog was through the door in a trice.

'No,' said Christian, 'I shall walk awhile.' The street was deserted, the shops and booths all closed and shuttered, and the air silent and still. Inside the hotel were music and light, but no sound or glimmer reached Christian as he went forward.

He had made what seemed to him good progress when he saw somebody coming towards him, stumbling and making small noises of distress. Christian was glad the dog was in the hotel for it grew impatient with people who moaned, and snapped at their ankles. He stopped and held out a hand.

'Who's that?' said the stranger. 'Who's there?'

'Only me,' said Christian, 'only me.'

'Oh, it's you,' said the stranger. 'I thought I was lost.'

'Who are you?' asked Christian, peering more closely.

'You know me,' said the stranger. He laughed deprecatingly. 'Everyone knows me. They call me Sudsy.'

He did look a little familiar, thought Christian. But then he looked just like a great many other people. 'Why were you crying?' he asked.

'I thought I was lost,' said Sudsy. 'I thought I couldn't find my way back. It was dark and there was no one there.'

Christian sighed.

'I'll walk back with you,' said Sudsy. 'That'll be all right, won't it?'

'I wasn't going back,' said Christian. 'I was going on.'

'Oh no,' said Sudsy, beginning to weep afresh.

'Come with me,' said Christian.

'I can't,' said Sudsy, 'I'm not ready. I'm afraid. When I left the village and all the people I knew I thought I could go on by myself, but I can't. It's too dark and there's no one I know out there. I want to get back to the place I knew, the people I knew.'

'I don't believe you can,' said Christian.

'You can,' said Sudsy. 'I've done it before, several times. I've set off and then gone back and they're all there – just as they were.'

'Don't you get bored?' asked Christian. 'Going away and coming back like that?'

'Not when they're all there,' said Sudsy. 'Not when I can watch them.'

Resignedly Christian turned, and as he did so a small figure sprang from the hedgerow beside him. 'Beware of pity,' it remarked, and sprang back into the leaves from where it sat and observed him interestedly. Christian hesitated.

'Come on,' urged Sudsy, 'they'll be gathering for the evening meal. We'll be able to see them through the windows.'

Christian went along beside him, back to the hotel.

'Hoy,' called Sir John imperiously, at the hotel desk.

Death walked into the light. 'Sir?' he inquired.

'Key,' demanded Sir John.

'Your room is not locked,' said Death.

'What do you mean – not locked?' said Sir John. 'I locked it myself. I've got some very valuable stuff in there.'

'It is all quite safe,' said Death, 'more than safe.'

'Now look here . . .' began Sir John.

Christian's dog whined. 'I don't think it's any use arguing,' he said. 'I don't think it'll do any good at all. Not here.'

Sir John hesitated, looking a little bewildered. 'I'm paying enough for all this,' he said, 'the least I can expect is proper security. I'll have a word with the manager in the morning.' He turned towards the bar.

The dog looked up at Death and Death looked down. 'There isn't any charge,' said Death. 'Explain that to him.'

'It's all very fine and good,' grumbled the dog to himself, as he followed Sir John to the bar, 'but how do you explain that to a rational man?' He tried. He sat up with his bright, intelligent eyes on Sir John and said that the desk clerk had said that there wasn't any charge. Sir John laughed indulgently.

'You misheard,' he said. 'There's always a charge.' The dog didn't contradict him for he entirely agreed. He lay silently for a while, puzzling over the matter.

'What we want,' said Sir John, 'is some stimulating company.' He gazed round hopefully, though not expectantly. 'Bring on the dancing girls,' he said, catching the eye of a lady at a nearby table. She gazed back, and after a while, as he looked into her eyes, he saw not eyes but hollows, and they were very deep. 'Let's go out,' he said, having found this a most disconcerting experience. 'Let's go slumming for a bit. Dead-and-alive hole this is!'

'Make up your mind,' said the dog. 'You should've brought your dog,' he added. 'I'm staying here.'

'I don't need a dog,' said Sir John. 'I'm perfectly capable of looking after myself.'

The desk clerk and the manager stood watching as he left. 'For a moment there,' said the clerk, 'I thought he wouldn't be staying, but judging by his last remark he'll be back.'

'Oh yes,' said the manager, 'he'll be back.'

'It's the familiarity I like,' Sudsy was explaining. 'The signature tune, the characters, the landscape.' Christian looked inquiring. 'I feel at home here,' continued Sudsy. 'I understand the regulations.'

'What regulations?' asked Christian.

'He means those imposed by the genre,' said his dog, who had been waiting for him, assuming confidently that he would be back.

'You've lost me somewhere,' said Christian.

'Then ask him,' suggested the dog. 'Ask him to put you in the picture.'

'Put me in the picture,' said Christian to Sudsy.

'It'll be more boring than if he was telling you his dreams,' said the dog, whispering into Christian's ear. 'A person telling you the plot of his favourite soap opera is more boring than anyone. Are you sure you can bear it?'

'I'm interested,' said Christian.

'You won't be,' said the dog. 'The third most boring thing is being told the plot of a soap opera.'

'What's the second?' asked Christian, unwisely.

'Have you forgotten?' said the dog, wearing the annoying expression of one who knows more, by dint of using his memory, than his interlocutor. Even the most aware and intelligent being is at a disadvantage if his memory deserts him.

'I don't think I ever knew,' said Christian, in order to confound his dog and his memory.

'Yes, you did,' said the dog. 'It's travellers who tell you how everywhere they go reminds them of somewhere else. You've done it yourself. You said Port Said reminded you of Llandudno, and the Dordogne reminded you of Devon, and Amsterdam reminded you of Hell.'

'I've never been to Hell,' said Christian.

'Sure?' asked the dog, pertly. 'Where are you now?'

'I don't know,' said Christian.

'That's quite a good definition of Hell,' said the dog, and he lay down on his side.

'Well, I know I'm not in Amsterdam,' said Christian.

'You can't even be sure of that,' said the dog, lazily.

'Where am I?' asked Christian, turning to Sudsy.

'Here with me,' said Sudsy. 'Here in the centre of everything.'

Christian looked round. He saw only the interior of the hotel; and the windows were dark and blank. 'Tell me,' he said.

'Well, up there on the hill,' began Sudsy – Christian looked through the window but could see no hill – 'there lives the squire and his son and his secretary and a woman.'

'What woman?' asked the dog.

'I'm not sure,' said Sudsy.

'Why not?' asked the dog.

'I missed a few episodes,' said Sudsy. 'I had to do something else.'

'What?' demanded the dog.

'Stop interrupting,' said Christian, who could tell already that this account was indeed going to be boring and wished the storyteller to hurry up and get to the end of it.

'I like to get things clear,' protested the dog.

'Constant questioning is not the way to get things clear,' said Christian.

'Yes it is,' said the dog, outraged at this dismissive attitude to his whole purpose in existing.

'You'll never hear the answer that way,' said Christian, 'and, what's more, you'll never hear the full story.'

'I don't believe he knows the full story,' said the dog.

'To be honest,' said Christian, 'nor do I, but let him tell it in his own way.'

'It's so sad,' said Sudsy, beginning to weep again, 'and I don't know what the ending is.'

'So what was the beginning?' inquired the dog.

'The word,' said Christian suddenly.

'Oh, very revealing,' sneered the dog. 'Very illuminating. What happened next?'

'It's been going on for a long time,' said Sudsy, sniffing. 'I remember it started badly but then it got better for a while and then it started going off again. I know the son was down here in town for a while. I wanted to see him. I'm a fan. I go to all the pop concerts to see the stars in person. It's my hobby.' Christian and the dog were both silent. Christian because he didn't know what to say and the dog because he was disgusted. 'It's all so familiar yet not familiar,' moaned Sudsy, 'like the way you dream of a room you're sitting in. They're not the same.'

'I know what he means by that,' said Christian with his hand over the dog's mouth. 'That makes sense.'

'Not a very great deal,' snarled the dog, breaking free.

'I think you should rest for a while,' said Christian to Sudsy. 'I think I'll go on now and I'll see you again later.'

'I'll miss you,' said Sudsy. 'I've enjoyed talking to you.' He looked lost and afraid.

'You sure you should leave him like that?' asked the dog cheekily. 'You being so good and so mindful of others and so on.'

'It's out of my hands,' said Christian.

'Oh, out of your hands, is it?' said the dog. He stood on his hind legs and minced around, jeering. 'Can't catch me,' it said, dropping on to all fours and leaping for the door.

'Come back here,' yelled Christian without thinking, used as he was to the animal's constant presence. He ran after it, knocking over a stool. Death watched him go but Sudsy only looked at the floor. A dark man sitting in a lighted corner watched him.

'None of your tricks, mate,' said a waiter affably as he passed with a salver of drinks. 'You've been barred once.' The stranger smiled.

'No one even knows I'm here,' he said. 'It's years and years since anyone even noticed me.'

'You were never written out of the script,' said the waiter over his shoulder, 'but that doesn't mean you can come in here when you like.'

At the word 'script' Sudsy looked up. 'Don't I know your face?' he asked in sudden excitement. 'Weren't you . . .?'

'Oh, once,' said the stranger idly. 'Haven't worked for some time. Haven't needed to.'

'You were the one in the black hat,' said Sudsy. 'I remember you now.'

'I kept them glued to the screen,' said the stranger complacently. 'I was good.'

'Words like that on *your* lips are not permitted here,' said the waiter. 'Out.'

'It makes no difference to me,' said the stranger. 'Where I go – as well you know . . .' and he was gone.

'He doesn't wash much, does he?' said Sudsy, becoming aware of an unpleasant smell. 'Fancy that, when he made so many commercials – for soap and scent and stuff. And he was always so well dressed. He had a great following.'

'He still has,' said the waiter, 'but we don't encourage him in here. He draws a lot of riff-raff. Lowers the tone. He's got his own place anyway. Don't you go getting mixed up with him.'

'He would've been someone to talk to,' said Sudsy wistfully. 'Someone to look at.'

Christian stood on the road. There was a great ringing in his ears and he wondered if he had had too much to drink: he had lost all concept of time and still barely knew whether it was light or dark. He didn't know which way to turn.

'Place is lively tonight,' said Sir John walking up to his side. 'Sounds like they've got the brass band out.'

'Where?' asked Christian. It seemed to him that the noise was lessening.

'Don't know actually,' said Sir John peering round. He had walked, looking for the source of the sound when he had thought it was music, but then when he couldn't find it he had thought of it as noise and gone back to the hotel to complain. All the members of the staff had smiled at his indignation, had been somehow remote from him, behind desk or bar or salver, and spoken politely. It had been oddly frightening and his wrath had faded as he left. 'Disobliging lot in that hotel,' he said. 'You going my way?' His voice quivered. Because of this Christian spoke kindly.

'I don't know,' he said. 'Which way are you going?'

'It's a funny thing,' said Sir John, 'but I've been from end to end of this place and it all looks the same. You can't tell right from left or north from south. Where's that dog of yours? Dogs have a good sense of direction usually.'

'I noticed that,' said Christian. 'How confusing it is, I mean. It's rather like Bala. I could never remember which end was which in Bala.'

'You're doing it again,' said a voice from low down. 'You're making absurd and unrealistic comparisons in the attempt to orient yourself.'

'Oh, hullo, dog,' said Christian resignedly. 'I thought you'd run away or got taken to the pound.'

'Me?' said the dog. 'Me run away? Never.'

'You've done it before,' said Christian. 'You've abandoned me before now.'

'That was different,' said the dog.

'Never mind that,' said Sir John. 'Can you show us the way?' The dog lay down in the road.

'I don't know,' it said.

'What do you mean you don't know?' cried Sir John. 'You're a dog, aren't you? You're supposed to know that sort of thing.'

'I have never,' said the dog magnificently, raising its head, 'denied my limitations.'

'You have,' said Christian crossly. 'The way you used to go on anyone would've thought you were omnipotent. What use are you now?'

'Yes, well . . .' said the dog, laying its head down on its paws again.

'Then let's go back to the hotel. We can ask there for directions and sit down and think about it.' Sir John started to move. 'When we can see what we're doing we could toss a coin.'

'I told you you should've brought your own dog,' said the dog.

'I'm beginning to be glad I didn't,' said Sir John, 'for all the help you're being.' A light suddenly bloomed above his head. 'Ah,' he cried, 'now we can see our way a little.'

'The hotel's just behind you,' said the dog.

Sir John spoke to Death at the desk. 'I want another room,' he said. 'I want a better view. I'm not satisfied. When it's all arranged you'll find me at the bar. Oh, and tomorrow I shall be going for a round of golf followed by a bathe in the ocean. Fix that at the clubhouse, will you.'

Death spoke to a minion in the shadows behind him and Sir John thought he heard them laugh. He spun round wrathfully but Death looked as though butter wouldn't melt in his mouth. 'That will be all right, sir,' he said.

'I'm not sure about that lot,' grumbled Sir John to Christian. 'Insolence in the staff is something I will not tolerate.'

'Quite right,' agreed the dog, sniggering. 'You tell them.'

'What I don't understand,' said Christian, 'is that when I first came near this place I thought it was quite a small village. Why is there a hotel this size here? You wouldn't think there'd be the custom.'

'Small?' said Sir John, astonished. 'Didn't you come in by the airport? It's enormous. The biggest I've ever known. Hundreds of terminals. The noise was unbelievable, the people – I've never seen so many in one place.'

'I came by boat,' said Christian uncertainly. 'I think . . .'

'Don't you *know*?' demanded the dog.

'I've forgotten,' said Christian shortly. 'There were quite a few of us at one time but then I found myself alone.'

'Well, you're not alone now,' cried Sir John bracingly and turned towards the hotel. 'What'll you have?'

Sudsy was alone. He was sitting in a corner staring at a television screen with the remote control in his hand, flicking it incessantly. Scenes of war and violence, of passion and sentiment, of gaiety and sorrow, of cars and money and margarine and soap powder flashed briefly before his eyes and were gone.

'The boss doesn't like them watching that,' whispered one waiter to another.

'He doesn't mind when they've really got nothing else to

do,' whispered back the second, adjusting his wings beneath his jacket, preparatory to sallying forth with a tray of canapés. 'That one's getting bored with it already. He'll give it up when he sees it's no use.'

'Just as long as he doesn't watch the news,' said the first waiter.

'He can't tell the difference,' said the second.

Christian was ill at ease. The dog was lying heavily on his foot and he was not interested in Sir John's talk of money and golf. The other people around seemed enclosed in private preoccupation. There was nothing to hold his attention and he was conscious only of a great yearning to be out of there and away, to be out in the garden.

'Is there a garden here?' he demanded of a passing waiter.

'What sort of garden would you prefer, sir?' asked the waiter. 'Tropical? English country? Stately house? Japanese? Rock? . . .'

'No,' said Christian and was disconcerted by his own swift response. The garden he wanted was none of these.

'We passed a garden on the way here but I wouldn't let him go in,' the dog told Sir John complacently. 'It didn't welcome dogs. I would've had to be retrained and you know me – I like my own way.'

'Shut up,' said Christian, 'you horrible, unruly, disobedient, misguided cur.'

'Charming,' said Sir John and the dog bristled offendedly.

'Shall I make him a garden?' asked a young member of staff rattling a seed packet.

'He wouldn't be fooled by it,' said the manager thoughtfully. 'He'll be leaving before long,' and indeed, already, Christian was getting to his feet with the look of a man about to take his departure. He spoke to the bartender on his way out.

'Give the dog a Pernod,' he said, 'a double.' He crossed the road and entered the inn. 'Which way?' he asked of the innkeeper.

'Where's your dog?' asked the innkeeper.

'In the hotel,' said Christian, 'getting drunk.'

'Then it's up to you,' said the innkeeper. 'You'll find the way.' He put a loaf and a bottle of water in a bag and passed them to Christian. 'A little viaticum,' he explained. Christian bowed his head to express his gratitude and left.

It was silent now, the street deserted, but he walked on through the unreality towards the light of dawn.

It was some time later, or perhaps no time at all, when Sir John holed in one and the dog found a bone. They walked to the shore but the sea was rolling away.

'Tide's going out,' said the dog and Sir John said he wasn't satisfied.

The sea rolled away out of sight and there was nothing but emptiness.

'I think I've got a hangover,' said the dog. 'I think, therefore I have!' It started to rehearse its conjugations: '*Être*,' it began, '*avoir*', and howled as the darkness descended.

A TALE FROM KASHMIR

I was told this story by a cab driver from Kashmir. We were driving in Yorkshire at the time.

There was an old man whose wife had died. He lived with his son and daughter-in-law and his little grandson.

One day his son's wife said to her husband, 'Your father is driving me mad: by day he is always under my feet and all night long he coughs so much that he keeps the child awake. You must send him away.'

The son was horrified at this suggestion. 'My father?' he cried. 'Send my father away? How can I? He is my father and I love him.'

'It is either him or me,' said his wife. 'Either he goes or I go.'

'But . . .' said the son. 'But, but, but . . .'

'Him or me,' said his wife.

The next day the young man took the old man up on a cliff top. 'Father,' he said, 'it breaks my heart but my wife says you keep the child awake with your coughing and I am going to push you off this cliff top. I have to do this or she will leave me.'

First the old man laughed and then he cried.

'Nothing you do will turn me from my purpose,' said the son, 'but first tell me why you laughed.'

'I laughed, my son,' said the old man, 'because fifty years ago I pushed my own father off this cliff top.'

'Oh,' said the son after a moment. 'But tell me now – why did you cry?'

'Because,' said the old man, 'I love you, my son, and fifty years from now your own son will push *you* off this cliff top.'

'What happened then?' I asked the cab driver. He said he didn't know, but he liked to think that father and son had gone home together and spoken reasonably but firmly to the woman of the house.

I said I hoped that had happened too.